D0934779

The Rape
of Shavi

Buchi Emecheta

George Braziller, Inc.
New York

Published in the United States in 1985
by George Braziller, Inc.

Originally published in Great Britain by Ogwugwu Afor Co., Ltd.,
7 Briston Grove, Crouch End, London N8 9EX and Umuezeokolo,
Ibuza, Bendel State, Nigeria

LIBRARY OF CONGRESS CATALOGING IN PUBLICATION DATA

Emecheta, Buchi.
The rape of Shavi.

I. Title.
PR9387.9.E36R3   1985   823   84-27424
ISBN 0-8076-1117-4
ISBN 0-8076-1118-2 (pbk.)

Printed in the United States of America
First edition

To
Chisingali and Ngozi Emecheta is dedicated this imaginary story
of imaginary events in an imaginary country of Shavi

Contents

The Rape
of Shavi

1
The Bird Of Fire

It was good to rest after such a long drought. King Patayon
had thought it was going to carry every man, woman and child
away to their ancestors. Evidently this time the ancestors had
not been ready to receive them. Even to fifty-year-old, slow-
thinking and easy-going King Patayon, descending to the
ancestors, however beautiful Ogene the river goddess had said
it was, was not a rosy prospect. Not that he distrusted the prophets and priests of Ogene, it was just that nobody had been to
the ancestors and back to tell them what it was like. The priests
and prophets claimed that the dead ones spoke through them,
but King Patayon, indulgently called "the Slow One" by his
subjects, sometimes had his doubts. The priests and the prophets were very useful in instilling fears into the minds of the
people of Shavi, by adding a tinge of the supernatural to everything. So the King was not going to go out openly and ask the
people, "But how do we know the dead really do speak through
the priests?" They were doing their work, and he was doing
his. And on a day like this, when everything was working as
expected, why should he complain?

It was blissful to sit with one's advisers, reminisce leisurely
about the past, and ponder a little about the future. For the
present, there was plenty to eat and the children were in excel-
lent health. The sun was going down in the west, the date
palms threw long, spindly shadows, and the palace walls fat,

robust ones, as if in competition. Among the shadows, colourful birds sang twitteringly in their nests. The palace parrots
hopped about in their cages, impatient with the twittering
birds. Even the King's bush cat sat lazily by its master, looking
from one end of the vast palace compound to the other, or
stretching and letting out a watery yawn before starting to lick
himself. From the nearby lakes, which had decided the found-
ing fathers to settle here in Shavi, and given them their goddess
Ogene, water, and fish, a breeze wafted over the palace walls
through the date palms and onto the king and his closest
friends, reclining together in the piazza.

Two of the palace dogs started to bark at the same time, but
in that relaxed welcoming tone known to King Patayon, from
which he could guess that whatever was approaching was not
dangerous. One of his wives perhaps, or one of his many children, or a friend. There was no need for him to stir. He merely
changed from resting on one arm to the other, selected another
toothpick and started to rid the gaps in his teeth of the particles
of roasted goat he and his men had eaten for the afternoon
meal. He had hardly settled down to this, when he saw six of
his chiefs slowing making their way to the piazza. They
walked leisurely, looking very dignified, not only because it
was a restful afternoon, now bordering on early evening, but
also because they were chiefs, middle-aged, and, above all,
men. Middle age such as theirs demanded dignity. They were
not ruffled by the barking of the dogs.

The chiefs, as if they were one man, knelt on one knee,
moved their white body cloth from their shoulders to their
armpits, and bowed their heads. King Patayon smiled, inclined
his head in return and motioned them with his hands to get up.
He gestured them to their seats, and the chiefs, slowly but
with subtle calculation, moved, three to each side of the king.
They too reclined on the scented skins of animals that had been
scattered on all the elevated sitting places built into the inside

2

walls of the palace. Young boys, who worked in the palace as servers and bodyguards, padded in like silent locusts, distributing chilled coco-palm drinks, honeyed bushmeat, nerve-relaxing grass, jenja nuts and eggs. Despite their busy air, not a word was spoken.

King Patayon, known as the Slow One, hated approaching any topic in haste. After a quarter of a century of his reign, his men had come to value this and to accept these long communicative silences as the behaviour demanded within the palace walls. The king knew his men came to the palace for a reason, though he didn't know what it was, but since they were using his own method in approaching the matter, he didn't wish to hurry them. So with them, he changed from reclining on one arm to the other, and gazed at the shadows lengthening along the palace walls.

As the silence was getting longer than usual, Patayon smiled into vacancy. His men had come to complain about something, something embarrassing, so they didn't know how to start. And he wasn't going to help them. The king and his men had sworn with their life blood that no one should oppress or use his position to treat the other subhumanly. They had learnt through their ancestors what it was to be enslaved, and Shavi prided herself on being the only place in the whole of the Sahara, where a child was free to tell the king where it was that he had gone wrong. And the child knew that not only would he not be punished but also that he would be listened to and his suggestion might even be incorporated into the workings of the kingdom. That King Patayon and his fathers before him had been able to do this and still retain their respect and dignity, was always a marvel to other kingdoms around.

Then, as if on cue, one of the men started to talk banalities. King Patayon, the Slow, smiled again and joined in the spirit of the game. Then there was a rustle, subtle yet determined, from the part of the palace that belonged to the King's wives.

Patayon, who had eight of them, and was about to marry a ninth, knew from experience the rustle of each woman's waist wrap and body cloth. He could tell that that particular nervous rustle was coming from no other than his senior wife, the trouble-maker and great talker, Shoshovi. Now King Patayon was ruffled. For it was one of the prerequisites of respectability in Shavi that a man must be capable of keeping his house in order. The approach of this woman, with her long and rather undignified strides like a man's, spelt trouble. The languid smile disappeared from King Patayon's face and in its place came a fixed grin. He sat up with deliberate slowness, and for once, the stress of ruling over twenty thousand people and of making sure that his family was a model of respectability showed slightly on his face.

The Queen Mother, Shoshivi, did not look at her husband's face. She made straight for the centre of the gathering and knelt in salutation: "I greet you, our King and our owners."

"Get up, Shoshovi, you know you're always welcome to come to the gathering of men at any time," King Patayon said cynically.

The King's men noted this, but wore faces so blank that they were almost mask-like.

The King's big cat, Kai-kai, left its master's side and walked slowly to Shoshovi, purring and rubbing its big overfed body against her. She started to stroke him as she got to her feet. She felt like holding the cat for reassurance but it was too big and heavy, so she clasped her hands to her front and looked over the heads of the reclining men. Not that they would kill or harm her if she said something stupid, it was just that in a place like Shavi, people knew so much about each other that shame killed faster than disease.

"My owners," she began, "I invited you to the palace for a purpose. You all know what they say, that women are the softness on which our men recline. But sometimes that softness

4

has gently to give a reminder to our men and our owners. I beg you all to go to the heart of the matter, to tell your friend and your King why it is that you are here. For if one's friend behaves badly, one is not entirely without blame. Ogene our goddess says that we are all responsible for each other, and forbids that we should let the communal spirit die and go back to the way our people were forced to live in Ogbe Asaba.''

The men all beat their left sides, nodding as they chorused gravely, ''Ogene forbid!''

As usual there was a long trembling silence, broken only by Kai-kai's loud purring. Then the King looked at all his men, his eloquent silence demanding explanation from them. His eyes rested on his oldest and most trusted friend, Egbongbele, who shifted from one arm to the other in embarrassment. He coughed and began to speak.

K R.

''Our Queen Mother's grievances are not unimportant. For is it not known that if one's women are contented, life will offer one contentment?''

Patayon broke in, coolly, ''You are free to get on with it Egbongbele. This is a free kingdom. And sometimes things do happen in one's own home of which one is the last to know. No person in Shavi should be afraid to speak to the King. Even Shoshovi is speaking her mind.''

Egbongbele didn't know what to make of this statement, so he delegated the nasty job to a young member of the group who was well known for tactlessness.

''Mensa, stand up and tell the king where he's gone wrong.''

A young and over-enthusiastic man, in his early thirties, got up with jerky energy and spat, ''The King must give Shoshovi a cow before taking the beautiful and dutiful daughter of Ayi to be his ninth queen. Shoshovi wants a cow.''

Lithoko

Egbongbele now looked very confused and Shoshovi started to wring her hands. Why let the tactless Mensa speak to King Patayon like that? What were these men up to? Trying to amuse themselves at her expense? Trying to trivialise her anger and her pride? "Shoshovi wants a cow", just like that, as if she was a lion hungry for flesh. They were well behaved enough not to laugh, but she knew that they were laughing in their hearts and that her husband, King Patayon, was laughing the loudest behind that noncommittal face. She felt humiliated, ridiculed. To march out of the gathering was her first impulse, but such ungracious behaviour was not expected of the King's wives, to say nothing of the Queen Mother herself. For, being the first wife of the reigning King, having seven younger wives after her, and being the mother of the King's heir, Asogba, was she not the Queen Mother? Her life and position demanded calm and compromise.

Shoshovi had her argument clear in her head, and no amount of ridicule was going to make a thing she had thought out so clearly look and become ridiculous. She stood there, her arms held tight to her front, her head held high, helped by her close fitting ehulu neckband, made from the precious glistening stones found underneath the foot of the hill by the Ogene lakes. Only the king's women were allowed to wear these ehulu neckbands. She had four layers which helped in propping her chin up. A queen was never seen outside her house door without the band. She had to wear it until the day she died. She now concentrated her gaze beyond the palace wall, where the dome of the palace buildings stood in silent silhouette against the sky.

The King's best friend, Egbongbele, was laughing again, this time foolishly. The shame and embarrassment was now theirs, not hers. She had presented her case as befitted the queen mother, and it was left to them to treat it as befitted the King's men. If they had set out to embarrass her, they had misfired. Her determined toughness and calmness were calculated to rattle them too. And she knew that her husband, King Patayon, couldn't help them.

The rest of the kingdom called him "the Slow One" and he didn't encourage people to think of him otherwise, but she, the woman who bore him his first son, Asogba, who had seen him cry when his father King Kofi died, had seen him doubt himself many, many a time, knew that behind that overplayed slowness was a mind that worked very fast and calculated rapidly. She waited.

"Mensa," Egbongbele stood up and began to clarify, "put it rather crudely. What our Queen Mother, Shoshovi, is saying, my King, is that you have forgotten to come to her house and tell her your intention to marry the gentle daughter of Ayi. She said she heard about it from the other queens when she saw the arrangements being made all over the palace, and didn't know what those arrangements were for. It looked as if a new bride was expected, but how come she wasn't consulted? We are now requesting our King to consult her in the proper manner with a well-fed cow."

King Patayon took the trouble to lift the lids of his eyes and look at his wife, Shoshovi. This dry stick of a woman with shrunken breasts! He studied the two bones that held her neck to the rest of her body, which started from each part of her jaw, and dipped themselves into her neck, forming a bony triangle. Her teeth, which were once very white and one of her beauties, now had black gaps between them. She was still thin as previously, but this new juiceless thinness was that of old age, with most of the nerves of her body going crisscross, almost in relief. Why had she become like this? Was it because she was now given to talking to herself in monologues and that whenever she opened her mouth, it was invariably to nag, to criticise? She had made herself unlovable by the bitterness that poured from her mouth.

Patayon didn't like the idea of any of his wives or any member of his household exposing him in this manner. But it would be silly of him to show his hurt. He didn't like the way

Shoshovi's case had been given to tactless Mensa to present to the King's friends. Surely Egbongbele could have chosen someone respected in the council of the Elders? It looked as if Egbongbele was making a joke at his expense. If Patayon had not tried his friend of many years, Egbongbele, several times and found him as steadfast and as unmovable as the rocks that guarded the Ogene lakes, he would have doubted his reasons for this undignified behaviour. But he knew that this was a mistake.

Maybe Egbongbele thought he would be pleasing his old friend by ridiculing his troublesome wife Shoshovi, but had forgotten that the people of Shavi said, "If a woman asks you to beat her badly-behaved child for her, one knows that those words do not come from the woman's heart". Only a silly person would take such utterances literally. This shows that one's best friends do not always know one thoroughly. Shoshovi was a troublemaker, but Shoshovi was his first wife, his first queen that his father King Kofi had married for him, and was Shoshovi not the mother of Asogba?

King Patayon's glance involuntarily went to Asogba who was leaning against an egbo tree, chewing something angrily. Like his mother his gaze was directed over the top domes of the palace and into the sky and somehow by this attitude of remote arrogance, he managed to reduce everything being said to a kind of irrelevance. Patayon knew that those eyes looking into distant vacancy missed very little. But how was he to know the way he felt about the treatment his mother was receiving from his advisers? Shoshovi should not have come here to complain about such a domestic issue.

Women! When they are angered, they forget how deeply they have loved. They throw all caution and reason into the empty air. They don't mind who they hurt in their search for justice. Patayon, who had loved Shoshovi, was suffering; Asogba, the son who would supercede him and who was borne

8

to him by Shoshovi, was suffering too. All for what? Simply because he wanted to celebrate the end of a long drought the way any ruler he knew of would, by taking a new queen. Now troublesome Shoshovi wanted a cow. He had been going to give it to her anyhow on the night of the bride's arrival. But he had been going to make sure that all the arrangements were made before he informed her. Now she had found out. Only Ogene knew what trouble she would cook up to make the going difficult for him. He would now have to use more pressure on the parents of the girl – a rather undignified move that would not befit a king. But what was there for him to do? Shoshovi should not have come to the gathering to expose him in this way . . .

A big, fast moving cloud suddenly loomed and tore itself from the sky, one minute a cloud, the next looking like an unusually long house, another minute the shape of a bird. It was spinning very fast, faster than any woman's spinning needle. Now it was smoking and coughing, and before the people could think what to do or say, the bird of fire arched and crashed into Shavi, just outside the palace walls, close to one of the Ogene lakes. The ordinary people of Shavi, the king, his men and their wives and children, every living thing, ran and hid.

"What is this? What has landed in our midst?" the people asked each other. "Has the Queen's anger become so great that she's summoned Ogene to send a mysterious bird of fire into Shavi?"

King Patayon gathered his loose body cloth and his wobbly body and ran. He ran in among the egbo trees, the tall cacti, past the palace walls, towards the biggest of the three lakes. There he knelt, his face distorted with fear as he prayerfully addressed the lake. "What is this monster that has descended on Shavi, Mother Ogene and all you goddesses of the lakes? What, or who are they, in that bird of fire? I will give Shoshovi a cow. I promise I will, but please, you ageless mothers, don't terrify your children so," went on King Patayon. But apart from the initial bang, nothing happened. King Patayon prayed himself hoarse. The tranquil Ogene remained calm. The egbo trees stood dignified in their thin stateliness, their stems naked and bare. The cacti shoots stood in humps like little ant hills.

As the air was now quiet, Patayon looked up to see a very curious diffusion of thick smoke melting into the clear blue stretches of sky above his head. The vast desert plain with its patches of cacti shoots lost itself in the horizon, until it met with the gentle incline of the hills surrounding Shavi like huge sentinels.

But neither plains, nor hills, could tell Patayon a thing. Maybe this phenomenon was beyond them, and beyond the Ogene goddesses. For how could Ogene and her sister goddesses, who for centuries had been worshipped and consulted by the people of Shavi in their sheltered desert homeland, dream of a bird that flew with a noise like thunder, a bird that had smoke in its tail, and carried human-like creatures?

Ogene did not answer Patayon. It was beyond her. This was something new, after which things would never be the same again.

2
The Leper Creatures

"Things will never be the same again." Patayon mouthed his thoughts aloud. And because he had said all he could think of saying, he started to listen. He could hear muffled cries of human suffering. When he sniffed, he could smell burning flesh. Patayon got up from his praying and peered in between the groves towards the area of the crash. He saw moving figures that looked very much like human beings, dragging one another from the fire. They were doing what anyone else would have done, but from where Patayon was painfully crouching, he couldn't swear to the fact that they were human. He had seen some animals do likewise.

He altered his position to get a better view. Yes, they looked like people, very much like him and his people of Shavi. But though he was still far from the place of the crash, he could feel that there was something strange about these creatures. Their clothes were odd, their colour frightfully strange, like the colour of lepers, and even their cries were as if somebody was holding their noses, making them emit sounds akin to the ones made by wild things when provoked. Nonetheless, they looked more like humans than animals, Patayon, the slow and dignified, decided eventually. But this was a discovery he was not going to make known until he had heard from his advisers, his priests and his people.

Meanwhile, what was he going to do? Trust that troublesome

11

woman to invoke Ogene to send leprous creatures in a strange-looking bird of fire. He had long suspected that the goddesses of the lakes always sided with the women. Shoshovi wanted a cow, and before he could think what to say or do, the impatient goddesses had sent these leper calamities, making funny noises and wearing even funnier clothes. Now everybody in Shavi was going to suffer, simply because of a stupid cow and a woman's jealousy.

Patayon waited, he knew not what for, adjusting and readjusting his body cloth. He shrugged his shoulders again and again, a sign that Patayon the Slow was thinking. He was muttering to himself intermittently, when suddenly a huge pile of leaves slithered up to him. Patayon jumped and shouted, ''Ogene, have mercy on us!''

''Oh, father, it's only me,'' Asogba announced, as he straigtened himself, rubbing the camouflage off his body. His usually lop-sided smile was so pronounced that Patayon couldn't tell whether it betokened derision or admiration. If Asogba had noticed that a minute earlier his father had been blaming the goddesses of Ogene for the falling of the bird of fire and was now calling upon them to save him, he didn't show it. He usually behaved likewise. When frightened, he would shout for his mother first, even though he agreed with his father Patayon that most women were created simply to cause men trouble. ''I want to go out and meet those people from the bird of fire,'' Asogba announced in harsh, hushed tones.

The rims of Patayon's eyes had never been so red as they were now. He opened and shut his mouth like the fish in the lakes. He was frightened, and was trying to transmit his fear to this rash son of his. ''Are you not afraid, young man?'' he asked at last. ''Is it not enough that your mother in her anger has invoked the Ogene to send us leprous-looking creatures in a strange bird of fire? Now you want to go and bring them into Shavi? Don't they look like lepers to you?''

"Is it like that, father? You mean these people come from our goddesses of the Ogene lakes? I never thought of that. And as for the colour of their skin, they look more like badly washed albinos than lepers to me, because they have no patches, father. I don't think Ogene's finished them properly and maybe she's brought them for our sun to finish them off...I don't know, but I want to find out."

They were both silent, thinking. Asogba flattened himself against an egbo tree, staring and squinting at the place of the crash so as to get a better view. When in thought, his face contorted like his mother's, his brows corrugating in deep furrows that made him instantly look older than his twenty-two years. He would emphasise his contemplative mood by placing a finger over his thin lips as if about to blow a whistle, peering out from dark lashes that looked artificially blackened. Once he had made his mind up, the furrows would smooth themselves out, the lopsided smile would spread across his thin lips, curiously progressing into a near vacant cheeky grin. That grin, sometimes resorted to to cover up embarrassment, and sometimes used as a bland senseless gesture, had never ceased to annoy Patayon, first in his wife Shoshovi, and now inherited in an exaggerated way by Asogba.

"It's not funny, Asogba. This is all your mother's doing, and you know it," Patayon snapped.

"Yes, father, but suppose these people are in danger, suppose they're refugees from slavery, like our great, great grandfathers all that time ago? Suppose they need help? Ogene would never forgive us, would she? Remember, father, you taught me that we're all refugees, immigrant strangers on this earth. We come and go like waves, you used to say to me, remember? So, why will you not now let me answer the cries of another set of refugees?"

"Asogba, I didn't ask you not to go," began Patayon, trying to regain his slipping dignity, "only that I have my doubts as to whether those figures are human or not. If they aren't, then they have no souls, and why should we pity figures that have no souls, which might be dangerous animals for all we know?

"Oh, father, I've watched them closely whilst standing behind that egbo tree, and I'm convinced that they've had a very bad accident. It even looks as if one or two of them are dead already. They feel pain, they talk, they walk on two feet. What other evidence do you want them to produce to show that they're human?"

"Asogba, what other human have you seen of that colour? What human have you seen flying birdwise like these ones? These creatures flew in here!"

Asogba was silent and the knowing grin on his face disappeared. His father was right. Only birds or animals of the air flew, not humans as he knew them.

The two men stood facing each other. It was uncommon to disobey a reigning king, and the king, knowing this, was extra careful not to put himself in a corner where any of the people he ruled might be inclined to go against his wishes. And now, to be so challenged by no less a person than his own son! To save face, Patayon mumbled, "I'm not ordering you not to go, but I'm advising you against it, as any other father would advise his son and heir".

There was no other way he could stop his son. The people of Shavi would resort to physical means of persuasion only as a last resort. They believed in talking an evil person out of his bad ways. They also believed that shame kills faster than any disease or physical harassment. Being such a close-knit society, they could leave the wrongdoer to his own conscience. The only punishment given was that of taking a life for a life, and they regarded honour, personal dignity, as life. For, they asked, if one's honour and dignity are taken from one, then what is left of the person? And any one who kills another person,

14

whether in anger or not, must forfeit his own life. This again
was as a result of what they had suffered when they were once
slaves in King Kokuma's land. So, other than ordering his
own son killed, there was no way of getting him to obey. He
would leave him to his conscience which would surely prick
him as to whether it was right to question a king's authority.

But Asogba's conscience worked differently. For the first
time in his whole life, nearly twenty-three years, he was
becoming impatient with his father's slow-moving ways. He
was beginning to have had enough of this man, who, though
his father, was nonetheless so slow, and who because of his
younger wives took a kind of negative pleasure in humiliating
his mother...

Suddenly, a piercing shriek rent the desert air. It seemed to
make the spindly leaves on the egbo tree quiver and go suddenly brown, and the hair of every human nearby stand on
end. Asogba peered through the gap formed by the two naked
branches of the egbo trees he had been leaning himself against,
and the sight that greeted his eyes made him want to cry.

He faced his father squarely. "That is the cry of a mother.
Look, she's carrying her little one, and I think the child is dead
or dying. I must go and see if they need our help. We must talk
about their humanity later."

With that, Asogba padded through the dead twigs and dying shrubs into the open space where the water-coloured bird
of the sky had landed.

"Why won't he let one of the palace guards go? After all,
he's going to rule," Patayon said aloud, thinking that he was
alone and talking to himself.

But he soon stopped as he noticed that the leaves that had
been still were moving and egbo trees started to dislodge men
form behind them. His men, who had flattened themselves
against the trees, apparently hadn't missed a word of the battle
between father and son.

"Maybe he needs to show the people of Shavi that he can rule without fear when you're gone, our ruler," Egbongbele felt bold enough to say.

"I'm not going yet, my friend," Patayon retorted.

Egbongbele heard, of course, but acted as if the King hadn't spoken. He turned and addressed the men, "Everyone go back to his egbo tree; you should all have your arrows fully saturated with poison and point them unwaveringly at the place of the crash. That way we will cover our prince, without making him lose face. He should not know of this because going there to face those strange creatures demanded the bravery found only in those of royal birth. We should be proud of him."

The king's men took their places behind the egbo trees, their arrows poised ready to fly, watching every movement that went on in the sandy centre of the place of the crash. They all, including Patayon, felt instinctively that the bird of fire heralded change. Whether good change or bad, only Ogene could tell.

3
The Song Of Freedom

The silence that reigned after Asogba's footfalls had died away made everybody introspective. How come the Ogene priests never foretold this event? They who were supposed to know everything. And how come his own dead father, who was always called the Wise One, never saw a day like this? His father, King Kofi, had told him the story of their ancestors, he had seen to it that the palace kriors sung it to him right from the time he could understand things. His father before him had done the same, and he, in his turn, had told it all to Asogba, who now was proving to be the inquisitive one. The kriors had beaten and sung the Shavi song of freedom every day, so that every child could intone it, however tuneless and unformed their voices were. They could sing:

"Hear the voices of Shavis singing!
Singing, singing the song of freedom.
They sing, they sing, the freedom song,
They sing to say to great King Kokuma
'Keep your protection and your gong,
For we want to be our own master, and protectors'.
Hear the voices of the Shavis singing,
Singing the joyous song of freedom."

Their ancestors had been enslaved by several kings called the Kokuma, somewhere over a hundred and ten days journey from Shavi. Whenever there was any sacrifice to be made, the

king would send for a son or daughter of the group of people
living in a place called Ogbe Asaba. The poor victim would be
killed, and, as this had always been the custom, it never occurred to anyone to question it. They worked for the king without any kind of payment, and were encouraged to breed simply
for sacrificial purposes. This unthinking way of life went on
until a boy, Shavi, was born, to a young girl who, legend
claimed, was once the king's sweetheart. The king wouldn't
marry her, not even to make her one of his lowest queens,
because she came from Ogbe Asaba. On pain of death she had
to keep her existence and the identity of her son Shavi quiet.
Everybody in Ogbe Asaba knew the story of the young girl
who was to be sacrificed for the drought, and how as she cried
to the skies to save her, it suddenly started to rain. Her life was
spared, but the young prince, Kokuma's son, had found her
unnaturally attractive. Though the boy Shavi lived and grew
in Ogbe Asaba, he was allowed certain privileges. The king
sent him a goat every year to celebrate the yam festival with his
mother. He was given proper body cloth of good quality at the
appropriate time, almost like the princes that lived in the palace
of King Kokuma.

When his mother told him why he was being singled out for
this privileged treatment, Shavi naturally resented being
regarded as one of the kept slaves in Ogbe Asaba. "For," he
continually asked himself, "why should I be treated like a
slave?"

Presently, his real father King Kokuma died, and another
son, Kokuma Nta, came to the throne. If he had heard the
story of Shavi's birth, he was determined to ignore it as an un-
founded rumour. He wouldn't even give Shavi the privileges
his father had given him. Shavi bore these humiliations like a
solid man. In humiliation, he took young Ejema for his wife,
and she soon had two sons for him. Legend said Kokuma Nta
smiled indulgently when he saw that Shavi had wisely accepted

a wife from Ogbe Asaba, the slave village. That meant that, whatever claim Shavi had to the royal blood, would not be extended to his sons. The blood in their veins had been too diluted with the blood of generations of slaves. Shavi became even more bitter and sometimes talked murderously. He swore that Kokuma Nta, who had robbed him of his right, though he was his half brother, would always be his enemy. And, like any dangerous enemy, Shavi was determined to get his own back one day.

Presently, the spirit of freedom in Shavi, which came to him through the blood of the kings that ran in his veins, rose up. He called together the men of Ogbe Asaba, and said to them: "We must go to King Kokuma to bargain for our freedom!"

"How are we going to do that? He will kill us all. He owns us," many of the men present reminded him.

"He doesn't own me. We're of the same blood. And before the end of my life, I must see to it that we're all free," Shavi retorted bitterly.

Many of the men present were bewildered. Some were rightly scared that the King, who had spies everywhere, might come to know of this meeting and punish them for it. Then, there was the problem of how best to cope with freedom. They had never been free before, had never gone out of their way to look for wives, or bothered to plan their lives, because the King had always done these things for them. He was the King, and he had therefore supernatural powers which they accepted must be placated by sacrifices, just as kings had to go at the call of Olisa. It would never occur to the King to say that he was going to seek freedom from Olisa, who gave him life. It was the same with them at Ogbe Asaba. How could they ask for freedom when they belonged to the King?

"Freedom is a difficult thing to possess. Many a time I have watched the kings, thinking and thinking about what would be the best for us and how to decide a case. They can do it because

19

they have the grace of the Olisa. And once people know that we are free, they are bound to start an attack on us, as we will no longer have Kokuma's protection. Freedom is a difficult thing," a wise one intoned, shaking his head sadly.

"The King will never let us go, anyway," declared another.

"And where will we go? The whole place belongs to the King," added a third.

"Listen, listen to me," Shavi cried, his arms raised. His kingly eyes shone and his voice was the voice of authority. A kind of hush descended on the group. Their eyes, which had been glazed to the point of stupidity with oppression, now looked up at him innocently, like the eyes of children.

They were all slaves, born of slave parents. A group of people trained to obedience without question. The free and fiery royal blood in Shavi confronted them, as it had never done before. They could think of no other protest. How could they? Had they ever had any cause to think for themselves? The Kokumas had always done the thinking for them, since anyone could remember. The king decided who was to be killed, who was to be sold to buy arms and amulets, which family should be allowed to breed and increase just for show, and now Shavi was questioning the very fundamentals of their existence.

"If we continue to be slaves, we'll go on losing our sons, our daughters and sometimes our lives. I'm offering you the opportunity to live free and die in ripe old age, as most people do. We're people too. We're not different. If you're frightened of the King killing us in the struggle, at least we'll die knowing that we fought for our freedom."

As a result of this meeting, the men of Ogbe Asaba sent a delegation to the King, which in itself had never been heard of before. It didn't take the King long to realise that the brain behind the scheme was that of his half brother, Shavi, the only man capable of thinking of freedom in Ogbe Asaba. No slave or any one born of slave parents would have done so. The King diplomatically agreed with the delegation. Then he asked, "But where will you go?"

"We will find land. We will walk and walk until we find a place of our own. The world is a big, big place, our King."

"But who will protect you against enemies, animals and many other perils? Freedom isn't easy, you know. You've been perfectly looked after all your life, so you have no idea what it's like to be on your own. Freedom is dangerous when given to those who have never been free before. You may even end up killing each other, just because I'm not around to stop such atrocities."

"We have considered all those things, our King, and we would still like our freedom. And we'll pay you fifty bags of kudos to buy it," Shavi added, as salve to the wound.

The young King and Shavi looked at each other, long and hard. Shavi knew that if his mother had not been from Ogbe Asaba, he, and not Kokuma Nta, would have been sitting on that royal stool, covered with the softest skins of animals. He noticed that the King had agreed too quickly. Shavi could guess from that look that it was not going to be easy. The other men were bemused by the King's apparent sincerity.

When the King agreed to take fifty bags of kudos from the slaves of Ogbe Asaba, he thought that it would take them years to save such a big sum, and he was going to make sure that they weren't given any free time to work for it. He was taken aback when only a few months later, the Ogbe Asaba delegation came again and offered the fifty bags of kudos.

The King called his men and asked them what he should do. They all knew that a king must never go back on his word. So they asked him, "Your Majesty, who owns the people of Ogbe Asaba?" The King replied that he owned them. So, they argued, if the King owned the slaves and the slaves owned the fifty bags of kudos, the King owned the kudos. Everybody knew that all a slave owned belonged to the master. The King

21

was very happy to hear this logic and he quickly put away the fifty bags of kudos and told the slaves what he and his men thought.

"But what of the freedom you promised?" Shavi cried.

"Freedom, freedom, are you not free? You are free to do what you like as long as you remember that I, King Kokuma Nta, own you. You may even take back your money and spend it the way you like, but I still own you. I allow you freedom in our great town. You may go now."

Shavi and the men took their money and began to make their journey home. Their hearts were heavy with sadness and they didn't know what they were going to do.

As if that wasn't enough, the King sent a messenger to the family of one Koku to come and visit him with his two sons. Koku knew what that meant. He knew that when they left the king's palace, his medicine men must have told him to purify the town of Kanene. They must have told him that for slaves to raise their voices in his reign and ask for freedom meant that the god Olisa was displeased with him, and to appease the god, some young men would have to be sacrificed. Koku and the other men had suspected that this would be the outcome of their audacity. He couldn't blame Shavi in his heart, and he didn't wish to make things worse by telling Shavi about it, because "If I do, the King may decide to take the rest of us as well". So, like a well-behaved slave, he went to King Kokuma. Also as a compensation, he knew that his son Foli would be a Kokuma in his reincarnation. Though he would have preferred his son to grow up to be a man with a family of his own, yet he told no one in Ogbe Asaba. He told the children only that they were going to pay King Kokuma a visit.

Whilst the king kept them in suspense in the open courtyard, Koku died many deaths in his mind. He never looked at his sons, not wanting them to see the fear in his eyes. He looked away and answered their questions with grunts. Eventually, Koku

22

was called into the palace building and requested to bring his first son. He went in, leaving the younger one outside in the courtyard. The boy was there until his shadow, that began the same length as his height, became longer and longer, and the sun went down in the west.

His father came out eventually, bowing and rubbing his hands together in gratitude and asking for the King's blessing on him. The King smiled benignly on the boy and shook his royal horse tail at him in salutation. Koku prayed for the King's long stay on the throne and beckoned his younger son to do likewise. The boy in confusion prostrated as he had been taught to do in front of royalty and got up only when the King said so. "What a noble family you have, Koku," the King had said. As the boy rose, he asked his father, "Where is my brother, Foli?" His father slapped him on both sides of his face, smiling a wobbly and apologetic smile at the King. "He is only young," he said.

Father and son walked away quickly to their homes in Ogbe Asaba. It was only when they got home that they could give vent to their feelings. Foli had been sacrificed inside the King's palace.

When, a few days later, the King sent for Shavi and his two sons, the people of Ogbe Asaba left that very night. And it was on the way to nowhere that they discovered, purely by accident, how to use the juice of the ewe tree as poison. They found out that if tips of arrows were dipped into the juice, it killed the enemy very quickly. Those sent by King Kokuma couldn't find them, as the people of Ogbe Asaba had learnt to stand very still behind trees and shoot poisoned arrows from their hidden places. Watching, unseen by Kokuma's men, they saw the last man leave. When it was night, they trekked and trekked. They wanted to make sure that they were as far away from Kokuma's land as possible. For over a hundred days, they trekked, stopping only to rest when the sun got too high.

23

Shavi, Koku and about thirty other grown-ups, and many children, walked a little each day, eating what they could find and killing animals for meat. Finally they came to a place, where the land was so flat, they could see for a long, long way ahead, where flowers were smaller but brighter and there was a dryness in the wind. Here they found it so cold they couldn't trek at night, as they used to. A further four days journey brought them to the Ogene lakes. They washed and made sacrifices, not with humans like Kokuma, but with birds. And because their prayers were heard and the lakes produced enough to feed them, birds became the object of worship of the people, who chose the name of Shavi for their new settlement.

Today, there were over twenty thousand of them. There had never been any killing. People prospered under democratic freedom, until the day when the silver bird blundered in upon them, shattering the tranquil atmosphere. An eel of fear in his entrails told King Patayon that from this day onward things would no longer be the way they used to be. Cold sweat covered him and he shivered. "Why, why should this happen in my time?" he asked the vacant air.

4
The Visitors

The flying group met on a cold, wet afternoon. The green grass on the Collingdale aerodrome was perfect, but the flowers edging the field were still uncertain what to do. It was early spring, but it looked and felt as if the winter of early 1983 would never end.

A small, curiously shaped aircraft stood motionless in the middle of the aerodrome. A man in his late thirties, in a duffle coat and mittens, stood by the aircraft, angrily stamping his feet and cursing intermittently. As he stamped, beating his body with his gloved hands, he shrugged and squared his shoulders, cursing the weather for being so cold and his friends for being late.

Presently, two figures appeared over the horizon. They were the figures of a woman, wrapped in a brown wool coat, pulling along that of a child dressed completely in red. On seeing them, the man stopped cursing and instead began to wave expansively, in the exaggerated welcome of the lonely. The way he behaved one would have thought that he had been waiting for his friends for hours, instead of fifteen minutes. The woman and child waved back: she with a controlled movement, the child with the natural exuberance of the very young. The child started to jump, to wriggle and struggle free of the woman's hand. She ran like a duck, her red poncho swirling this way and that. The woman's light laughter echoed over the aerodrome and was returned by the man's deep tones.

The child ran to the man, who met her halfway, picked her up and swung her round and round. The open space of Collingdale aerodrome reverberated with happy noises.

The man and the woman met. He kissed her on the cheek first, then on the mouth, both movements light and familiar. Then he remarked, "You taste nice and warm".

She smiled and tumbled her brown hair out of the hood of her coat.

"I was beginning to despair, I thought no one was coming." It was almost as if he was about to complain, but happiness glistened in his small blue eyes, now almost obscured by the smile on his broad face.

"Oh Flip, you're always like that, a born worrier, and invariably impatient with ordinary mortals like us," the woman observed indulgently.

"I didn't know what to think, to be candid," Flip said.

"You must have been waiting a long time them."

"Well, a little over fifteen minutes . . ."

The woman made futile attempts to cover her laughter, and Flip gave in to the urge to laugh at himself. They both laughed, and as a consolation, the woman added, "It's so cold. I wouldn't like to wait for anyone out here in the open on a chilly day like this. Let's go in, the others will be here soon."

The child, who by this time was skipping around the waiting aircraft, came round to the couple and announced, "Look, mother, mother they're coming. Dorf and his daddy and aunt Ista! Look, they're coming!"

"Oh yes, how clever you are, Kisskiss. Why don't you climb in with your mother and get the best place to sit before everybody else?" Flip said in amusement.

They both watched Kisskiss scramble up the metal stairs

that led to the waiting aircraft. "I should go in with her. Andria, if I were you."

"You're right, Flip. I dread to think what would happen if I left Kisskiss there all by herself."

Andria climbed the steep metal steps, and Flip watched her make her way safely inside before turning his attention to the three people coming towards him. They were a man and a woman, and trailing behind them, a boy of nine, who unlike Kisskiss and her mother Andria, didn't shout their presence. The boy couldn't run even if he wanted to, because he was carrying a satchel, a bat, and what looked from the distance like a small radio.

"What a cold day," breated Dr Ista Kidea. "Until yesterday, I was feeling sorry to leave the motherland, but I didn't know the motherland would force me away from her with weather like this. Whoo — just look at that."

All eyes followed her frozen breath whirling in the air.

"You'd better go in, young man," John Mendoza said to his son. "I can hear Kisskiss's voice from here."

"She's so childish, that girl. Why is she making all that racket?" Dorf asked.

"Well, young man, all women make a racket. Take that from your old uncle Fip."

"Stop that, Flip," Ista said, turning her fur-covered neck away from the men and marching up the steps into the plane.

Presently Tara, Moshem and Ronje, all members of the Newark flying club, joined the group and they all went in.

They got themselves strapped into their seats, while Flip taxied round the Collingdale aerodrome before taking off. Moshem, the twenty-nine-year-old aeronautical engineer, elected himself the steward.

"We have enough of everything," he boasted to Dorf and Kisskiss. "You name it, we have it on board."

27

"Do we have Kungfu ice cream with nutty chocolate all sprinkled over it and . . . lots of biscuits and chocolate . . ."

"You said chocolate before!" Dorf cut in exasperatedly. "Chocolate, chocolate!"

"We have enough chocolate to last us a very, very long time," Moshem affirmed, crinkling the corners of his eyes at the children in such a ridiculous way that Tara laughed aloud.

"Have we missed anything?" Ista asked from her back seat.

"We have an entertainer on board the Newark," Tara replied.

Moshem turned his face to the rest of the passengers and, crinkling the corners of his eyes, wiggled his ears at the same time.

The peals of laughter that followed could be heard by Flip in the pilot's cockpit. He smiled. The plan was working, Flip fell into a reverie as he flew.

As a child in his Sunday school days, Flip had always been struck by one of the miracles of Jesus, in which he had driven the devils from a madman into a herd of pigs that were grazing nearby. He had thought how odd that was. What would the pigs' owner do? Was it their fault that the man was mad in the first place? Another story that had intrigued him was the temptation of Christ. When He was hungry, Satan appeared to Him and said if He jumped down from the mountain, He would then be given all the Kingdom of the world and all the food He needed. Flip had since then dismissed the idea of the Devil living among human beings, or that he really existed. But how did you explain a Church Synod that endorsed nuclear power? God said, thou shalt not kill, but the Synod was saying, thou shalt. Flip, like many people who believed in God, was in a dilemma. What was there for them to do? This was what had led to his decision to try to preserve the great gift of life which God had entrusted into his care. He had persuaded some of his friends from the Newark flying club to escpae with him, and seek a refuge safe from the two warring giants.

Hours later, Flip was enjoying a deep sleep, when he felt a hand shaking him gently.

"Wake up, Flip. Do wake up," Ronje said in a hushed voice.

"What the h . . . !" He never finished the sentence. There was no need to swear, not when all was going as planned. Ronje smiled too, and gestured towards the pilot's cockpit.

"We feel something is really happening, judging from the reading on the binoark," said Ronje as Flip impatiently wrapped a lightweight house coat around him and followed the excited man to the cockpit.

"Just look at this, Flip," Moshem cried, his eyes no longer twinkling.

Flip took the instrument, a highly sensitive geiger counter, perfected by Moshem and to which they had given the name binoark. "Good Lord, that can't be the level of radiation surely! Have they pressed the button then? Let's watch it at a closer angle."

They could hardly contain their excitement as Flip fiddled with this knob and that knob of the aircraft's geiger counter. After a few minutes, Flip got what he wanted and the three men standing there simultaneously exclaimed, "Ah!"

The instrument showed a level of radiation far above the optimum: it meant destruction for all the people of their own world. They deftly piloted the Newark away from the affected area. They had known it was bound to happen, either by design or by miscalculation. Now they stared with near glazed eyes through the thick leaded glass of the cockpit, watching clouds glide slowly by, each wrapt in their own thoughts.

Moshem was doubting whether they had been right in seeking their own safety, rather than joining the campaigners against the nuclear pile up. What was life going to be for him without the mother he loved, his sisters, his uncles and aunts? They had taken so much pride in his success through high school, university, his training as a pilot, and his employment in one of the top defence ministries. Would the little communities he had known and grown up in in Holland, America and Israel be destroyed? What was now happening to his family. "Mother!" he exclaimed audibly and involuntarily, making the others jump. Their look challenged him for daring to say what they were all thinking.

"Funny. I was thinking of my mother too," Ronje said, in a low voice.

They were still engaged in a kind of wordless dialogue, when suddenly the Newark somersaulted, and for no foreseeable reason the power of the wind forced open the front top of the plane. It was as neatly done as if an invisible hand was playing a game with them. In no time at all, the most sophisticated equipment on board, their most reliable and sensitive hardware, the binoark, and bits and pieces of their survival kit, flew out with the wind force.

In the midst of the shock and confusion, Ronje managed to grope his way to the sleeping quarters and strap the kids to their seats. All was chaos and Flip at the controls could feel the wind toying with the part of the Newark that was still intact. He could hear shrieks of fear, as he saw something ahead like a lake and made for it.

Presently, he felt Dorf nudging him. He could also hear Andria shouting and urging all to clear away in case of an explosion. He thought numbly, "What a silly woman. Doesn't she know that the ark is proof against explosion?" Of course he would not leave the ark, wasn't he the captain? He could see some of the others, running along a white rocky place, a place so dry that the brittle cold air assailed the nostrils, as it had done before take-off only hours before. Or had it been in centuries long, long past? The other cold, dry place was heavily grassed, this one was full of dry sharp rocks. He tried to move his body, and he knew that, apart from a few bruises he would live. He could guess too that the daze he was suffering was the effect of shock. It would pass, if only he could rest his head awhile.

He had been one of the architects who perfected the nuclear bomb. Now he was running away from it to another part of the earth. He chuckled at his own stupidity. The stupidity of Jonah, running away from one's responsibility.

"Flip, Flip, please try to get up. The Newark could explode any minute! You simply have to get up, come on, I'm going to pull you out."

Flip found himself obeying Andria's urgent voice without thinking. He lifted his throbbing head. Damn Andria shouting like that. Couldn't she see that he couldn't move his head without pain? He heaved his body up with Andria's help and found himself staggering upright.

"Hurry, hurry, Flip, It may explode!"

He walked a few steps from the place of the crash, and felt his legs give way. As he fell, he heard more voices, but he could no longer think of anything except that someone should tell Andria that, though the Newark might be smoking, it would never explode. Then he permitted himself to drift into nothingness.

5
Members Of the Human Race

King Patayon gestured his men to have their poisonous arrows poised and ready to fly at his command. They maneouvred their sleek bodies into positions of advantage and were silent, still as the date palms that gave them protection. An untutored eye would never have guessed that behind each innocent date palm stood a man, dangerous with fear, ready like the rattle snake that frequented the area, to strike and kill.

The men of Shavi, and the women hiding in different places, could see all that was going on. They could see Asogba and could guess what he was saying to those strange creatures through his gestures. It was clear to them all even from such a great distance that they couldn't understand what Asogba was saying. The people were a kind of palish colour, stupid-looking, with their strange sounds, as if somebody was putting date palms in their nostrils. But Asogba the curious was not frightened. He was sure they were humans, because he could see one or two of them bleeding red blood, and one that looked like a woman crying, as women did when upset or frightened. What he wanted to know was why they should land in Shavi in this alarming way.

Meanwhile, King Patayon was thinking different thoughts. When his ancestors left Ogbe Asaba, they determined not to indulge in killing humans. It was a bird that led them to the Ogene lake, so after killing one bird in gratitude to Ogene for showing them the lakes, they had kept birds sacred in Shavi, killing only for sacrifice. Now these strange creatures had come in a bird on the day that the Queen Mother, Shoshovi, had been angry with her husband, King Patayon. What was he going to do? Suppose the creatures were human, and Ogene had sent them in a bird of fire as a sacrifice for the wrongs he had done his wife Shoshovi?

This last drought had carried away so many people. In the old days, the Kokumas ritually sacrificed humans after a long drought. Was that what the Ogene was trying to tell him, that these creatures should be sacrificed for her? "Oh, Ogene, why did you have to put me in this predicament?" he wailed inwardly. "The thought of killing a human being is appalling to me."

He looked to where Egbongbele was standing and saw to his satisfaction that his poised arrows never wavered. His steady eyes were fixed on his prince, Asogba. He did not look once at Patayon. Slightly ashamed, Patayon furrowed his brows in concentration and faced the place where the big bird had landed.

The creatures were now coming towards the palace walls, carrying different bundles. "Don't let them know our strength," Patayon said half aloud, as he extracted himself from the stillness. The message was relayed to Asogba, who promptly halted the progress of the approaching strange creatures.

The shadows were no longer giving the visitors a pitiable spindly image. There were seven of them in all. Two women, three men and two children. One of the women, the weepy one, was carrying one of the children. The men's clothes covered the legs like the shokotos of some horse and camel riders of Ongar. They came carrying their bundles, not on their heads like any sensible person would do, but in their hands. All these weighed them down and made their gait look rickety, despite the slanting sun. Poor beggars, away from wherever their home was.

Asogba halted, obeying the voice of the krior that had shouted to him from among the still egbo trees. The visitors stared at him uncomprehendingly. The woman carrying the child started to wail again and though Asogba wanted to laugh at the strange noise she made, he controlled himself. Even though he couldn't understand what she was saying, he knew that she was crying for the child she was carrying. One of the men offered to take the child from her, but she refused and wailed all the more. This puzzled Asogba. Perhaps they weren't humans after all. For why should one human wish to monopolise her sorrow, or even her child? People shared sorrow in Shavi, and any child is the child of the community. Maybe he was wrong. But he could leave the decision as to the humanity of these strange visitors to the priests and priestess of Ogene. They would know what to do. That kind of thing was their duty. If they could not tell for certain, then they would have to consult the Ogene goddess.

He directed his attention to the movements going on in the palace. He could see his mother darting this way and that, and his father's trusted friend, Egbongbele, hurrying to take his place by the Slow One, King Patayon. Asogba knew that he would have to apologise to his father for allowing his enthusiasm to get the better of him. He had temporarily forgotten the model of dignity expected in the palace. He had to give his father time to regain his position of respect.

Meanwhile, Andria lost her cool and started to talk to Asogba. "I must put this child down. She's just had a nasty shock, can't you see?"

Mendoza came nearer to Asogba and asked, "What stupid game are you playing on us? Why do you want us to wait here? I thought you were taking us over there, to where you live." He made as if to proceed towards the palace walls, but at once three or four palace guards swarmed on him. One gave him what was locally known as the camel blow, which doubled him up. He found himself sitting on the sand, moaning in pain like a child. Asogba smiled his lopsided smile and the others understood that they were being watched.

"You bloody bastard!" Mendoza groaned and Asogba smiled again, lopsidedly. He waved his arms erratically and told Mendoza that he had to be kicked, to give his father time to regain his position of respect, because the King of Shavi must never be caught unprepared.

"You bloody bastard. You signalled to your friends to come and kick me, didn't you?" Mendoza gave Asogba back in reply.

When Patayon was seated in his palace piazza, Asogba signalled to the creatures from the strange bird to follow him. When they came into the wide open space that formed the palace surround, the silence intensified. Even Andria, who had been complaining about Kinkins, was shocked into silence. Now they could see the people of Shavi clearly, Flip said under his breath, "It was a good thing we didn't give in to Mendoza and attack the young man that came for us".

Ronje looked around him and nodded. "You're right there, Flip."

When they came near the palace wall, Patayon gestured to Asogba to come near. He whispered in his son's ear, and Asogba's lopsided grin developed into a smile – a smile that was like sunlight suddenly illuninating a dark room. It was so infectious that Dorf smiled too. Asogba jerked his head towards the perplexed visitors, an indication for them to follow him. They did so, fearfully.

They passed through the palace walls, into the semi courtyard where they were made to walk in Indian file. Here were dwarf palms and date palms, giant crocus among which hens squawked and goats ambled. The date palms and egbo trees

35

afforded King Patayon and his men a shield. They watched the visitors as they moved, and King Patayon whispered to Anoku the chief priest. The priest nodded his skull-like head and intensified his scrutiny of the strangers. They made the leprous-looking people walk round the palace trees once more, until they were gestured to stop.

Presently Egbongbele, unable to bear the silence any longer, spoke up. "I think, my King, it would be proper to send our visitors to our guests' quarters. They look as if they need rest."

"We know that!" retorted Anoku, the priest with the skull-like head. "But how do we know that Ogene didn't want them sacrificed immediately? After all, they came in a bird – a sign that Ogene has something to do with their arrival."

"But I think they're human. Look at that child. It will die if we do nothing to help its mother. What type of people have we allowed ourselves to become, if we now start to kill people who are immigrant in our society instead of welcoming them?"

Patayon raised his hands. "We will not argue over this matter now. Asogba, you and the palace guards should escort the visitors to our best resting house."

"King Patayon, is it right to ask the prince to look after the creatures? Suppose we find out that they aren't human beings and that they have no souls? Our prince will have been contaminated." protested Anoku.

"I may not be a priest, and know very little about souls, but these people look human enough to me. They have legs, voices, and all our human features and they even cover their nakedness in strange-looking clothes. No animal would do that, not even our most tame monkeys. And if we have definite proof that they are humans, how will it sound when future people learn that we treat visitors or immigrants who land among us like animals? No, let the prince of the land take

36

charge of them. We are people who give the best to visitors. We cannot start changing that now. Take them away, Asogba, make them comfortable, and if it's proved that they're not human, we will have done our best." King Patayon relapsed into silence after this speech, which surprised many of his listeners by its emotion.

They all watched the people go in silence, disturbed only by Shoshovi, calling out loudly for the benefit of the sitting men to show that she was doing her duty. She summoned not only all the queens, but the new one: the fifteen-year-old Ayoko, whom all in the palace were training to be the first wife of Asogba. Ayoko trotted after Shoshovi as they carried bowls of food and water, and coconut butter to rub on the wounds of the visitors.

"I hope we're right," Anoku, the chief priest, grumbled after they had all left.

Mensa the great bungler got up again in his jerky way. The trouble with Mensa was that he was fond of doing his thinking aloud, thereby boring his listeners. The men of Shavi respected someone who did his thinking by himself, and spoke only when those thoughts were refined enough to be listened to. King Patayon would have preferred his men to go away and think about what they were going to do with the visitors. But Mensa the bungler was about to trivialise the whole issue.

And trivialise he did, much to King Patayon's silent amusement. "My King, men of Shavi, these visitors are people, just like us. The only difference is that they speak differently. I have seen lepers with that colour, but that doesn't mean that lepers are not people, does it?" he asked stupidly.

Iyalode, the priestess of Ogene, who had sat by the gate and listened to all the arguments, replied, "If we take innocent lives, we can't bring them back. I think our King, the slow and wise one, has taken the right course. Let us take care of them, until we learn their tongue. They are immigrants, just like us. They probably lack food in their country, or maybe they are persecuted as Kokuma persecuted us, and are political refugees. Let us watch them for a while. They may not even want to stay.''

Anoku, the skull-headed priest, was obviously upset that the arrival of the strangers wasn't being given a mystical interpretation. He worked himself up until the spirit of Ogene took hold of him, chanting and chanting until, near exhaustion, he started to speak plainly, so that the people of Shavi could understand. ''I see the Ogene river bubbling with blood instead of clear water. The Ogene is very angry. These people are not humans and will bring us destruction. They may look like humans but they have no souls. They should be used as slaves or killed or driven away. They will take advantage of our kindness and laugh at us, because they cannot appreciate kindness. They think it a weakness. They came on the day that the Queen Mother was upset, and they came in a bird to show that the goddesses of Ogene had sent them. If you people of Shavi want them to stay, then just remember that their arrival was symbolic.''

''Enough, enough'' Iyalode shouted, emitting a horrendous shriek that shivered the palace walls. ''Our heads are aching and you are beginning to rave like a madman, not like the great priest of Ogene.''

There was suppressed laughter on the faces of the dignified men of Shavi when they eventually raised their heads. Anoku's face was a picture. The bold voice of Iyalode had shocked him not a little, and anger had twisted his thin mouth into the shape of a desert snail about to crawl out of its shell, while it looked as if his right ear had pulled up the right side of his mouth. His ears, always too big for his hairless head, seemed even bigger. Anger and disillusionment can make an animal of any dignitary, even Anoku, one of the most respected men in Shavi. He got up in agitation, jerked his body cloth from one shoulder to the other, made as if he was about to speak, then decided against it, said "mesiere" to the council and marched out towards the Ogene lakes.

Silence reigned once more. It was never really decided whether the visitors were human or not, or whether they were sent by Ogene or the devil. If Anoku had had a point, his hysterical way of presenting it reduced it to the uncontrolled raving of a lunatic.

On the whole, the Shavi council regarded the visitors as humans, whose only difference was their pigmentation. So one by one, each council member promised to make the visitors feel at home. For, they said to each other, "Are we not all immigrants in Shavi, and even on the face of the earth? We're all members of the human race."

"And I think they're simply albinos. Did you see their eyes? One's were blue, another's the colour of water, and one's no colour at all. They're albino people," Iyalode, the priestess of Ogene, delivered after a short reflection.

This summary brought the matter to a temporary close. But Anoku the priest was still angry. And when the chief priest of a tribe is displeased, he can foretell many unpleasant happenings. But then his assistant the priestess had said that the visitors were only albino and since when have albinos stopped being humans?

6
The Cattle People

Dew hung white, thick and tangible on the face of the earth. It was so thick that they could hardly make out the outline of objects only feet away. It was cold as well. But despite all this, Ayoko knew that in less than two hours, the sun would gladden the earth, and melt the dew, making the day genuinely warm and then very hot. But until then there was mist, cold and chill.

She tightened her heavy morning osiba around herself, pulling one end past her ear under her chin to the other. Though all was still and there was hardly any wind, she didn't like the feel of the cold mist in her ears. The compound was quiet. Even the Ogene lakes didn't send out any breezes. It was so still, even the dogs in the palace didn't bark.

Ayoko sighed as she tightened her grip on the broom and started to sweep the palace compound. She heard the door leading to the visitors' house open, and looked up. Two scantily-clad figures came out of the door. Ayoko edged closer and could just make out the figure of Flip, whom they had all now learnt to call the head visitor, and the other man, with the big head, and little paunchy stomach, they called Ronje. Flip stood there in the cold, beating his arms about himself as if warding off flies, and trotting like a horse in the same spot. His companion with the big head was doing the same. After warming up, they started to run round and round their dome-shaped house. Ayoko thought this rather odd. Why should grown men come out of their sleeping places on a morning like this and start to run round in circles, like children at play? Why couldn't they sleep with their women as most men in Shavi would now be doing?

Ayoko knew that she too would be in the same position after the daughter of Ayi had settled as the latest of King Patayon's queens. Then the palace would start negotiating for her. But meanwhile, she was helping the Queen Mother, Shoshovi, look after the foreign visitors. She had to help in tidying the palace early this morning because the King would this day declare them people of Shavi. After today, Ayoko would no longer have to come every other morning to help in cleaning around their compound. They would be expected to do it themselves. She was still standing there, day-dreaming, when she heard running steps, near to where she was standing.

It was Ronje.

Ayoko almost jumped. But like all the women of the palace, she had been taught to keep her cool when confronted with danger or fear. So she pulled her head cloth down to her chin, almost covering her mouth and muttered, "Mesiere o", the Shavian greeting to friends.

Ronje, the hair on his body matted with sweat, grinned. "Mesiere to you, too. Do you have to wake up this early to sweep, poor girl? Here women are used as chattels, aren't they? Tell me, are you a slave or simply a serving maid?"

As Ayoko couldn't understand a word of what Ronje was saying, she simply smiled and nodded knowingly at the way he said his "mesiere", and went on with her sweeping. She wanted to tell him that from today they would be regarded not only as full humans but as free people of Shavi. But how could one do that to people who could speak only a few words of greeting pronounced in such a funny way? Their only other way of communicating was waving their arms up and down and opening and closing their hands. When she looked up, she saw that he was still standing there, watching her. She felt self-conscious.

She stopped sweeping, pointed her broom towards the door leading to the visitors' abode and said in her language. "I don't know why you're looking at me like that, making me feel silly. I saw you prancing about like a crazy dancer, with few clothes on. Go to your place of abode." Then she giggled. "To think my father still thinks you're probably non-human. Go to your house, man with the albino skin. I'm sure you are a man."

There was another sound of footsteps and they both turned round to see Flip puffing up to them. The sight of him made Ayoko laugh the more. "Why do you two prance about in the morning like mad people? If my father sees you, he's going to start saying that you're not human. What things you do!"

Flip said "mesiere" to her and turned to Ronje. "I thought you would have had your shower by now," he grinned dangerously. "You're been here all along chatting to this girl. Look out, old chap, she's only a child."

"I'm not quite sure of that. But what does it matter? After all, she's probably a slave or a sweeping girl of something."

"I don't think that's the point. We don't want trouble. Don't let us abuse their hospitality," Flip said cautiously, as Ayoko watched them go in.

Presently, the sun came out and the men of Shavi got up from their sleeping places to ponder on the big decision of the day. The men of the palace met very early, soon after the morning meal. They took their usual places by King Patayon, and everybody present knew more or less what he was going to say. The question of whether the visitors were human or animal did not arise. They had stayed a whole fourteen days, during which the people of Shavi had seen them eat, grieve and express the wish to bury their dead privately and with sorrow, allowing the grave diggers of Shavi to go with them. The little girl, whose mother had been hysterical with fear, had been healed through the gentle care of the women of the palace of Shavi. They had seen her gratitude. So why should they waste their time debating whether they were human?

When the priest and prophet of Ogene stood up to start his warning again, Asogba interrupted, saying that the people of Shavi should endeavour to find out how it was that the visitors could fly. All the young men, and the palace guards standing about, clapped and cheered him at this. The echoes of their joy went from one corner of the palace to the other. King Patayon smiled knowingly and gave only one glance to where his son was standing.

"It looks as if our young people have already made up their minds," Mensa remarked irrelevantly.

"Asogba, go and tell the high visitor, the one with hair all over him like an orang-utang, that he must go with you to the valley of the shepherds to get six cows. The best one should first be given to your mother, before we start the bridal celebrations."

All the men sitting around the King laughed.

So, Shoshovi is going to have her cow at last," Egbongbele remarked.

"I know, one would have thought that she saved cows to marry a wife of something. She has enough to give her all the milk she needs for her cooking and all the cows to celebrate all the festivals of Shavi for the next ten years. Women! At least, they have to be satisfied. My wife wants a cow before I can take a new wife, so please let her have a cow. Otherwise, she'll go and invoke her sister goddess of Ogene to send us more fire and bird-shaped monsters."

"I thought you didn't believe that Ogene had a hand in their arrival? I thought you sneered that their arrival was merely accidental, that I am an over-enthusiastic priest, prophesysing doom, just for the joy of it?"

King Patayon hated offending any of his men and especially the priests and priestesses of Ogene. He wished Anoku would not go on and on. He looked at his friend and ally of many years and arched his brow, as if to say, "Egbongbele, the ball is in your court. Deal with it."

Egbongbele cleared his throat to give him time to marshall his thoughts. The priests and priestesses must be carefully addressed. "Wizard of the birds, he who understands their language, and speaks for our great goddess Ogene, we thank you. We thank you and salute you for your guidance. We are sure Ogene had a hand in the arrival of these strange people in a flying bird. The fact that it happened on the day our Queen Mother was angry with our King as you know is symbolic. You have also heard our young people. Maybe Ogene sent them to teach us something. And if we kill them, then we will lose the culture they brought with them. Ogene taught them to fly in a bird, and she knows we worship her through birds, so she must have sent them to us. This is just my humble interpretation. But as for sacrifice, we have worshipped Ogene for the past five hundred years with birds, why should she suddenly come to have an appetite for humans? For I personally believe that they are human. Their colour is only skin deep. So, he who speaks with the voice of the bird, speak to Ogene for us. If we should kill innocent lives, Ogene herself will not be happy. Once more, our great priest, we salute you."

"Egbongbele, mesiere," the other chiefs said, with one voice.

Asogba walked jauntily into the centre, and saluted. "Mesiere, my fathers." He waited for them to reply to his greeting as a sign that they were prepared to listen to him.

"We have a busy day ahead of us, Asogba, with getting your mother her cow, and the King your father's bride to pay for, so that we can start the final talks about your future wife, Ayoko, the daughter of our great priest here," Egbongbele said

44

in warning, because he didn't know what Asogba was going to say. They didn't want to hurt Anoku more than necessary. He must be given enough room to make his social getaway.

Instinctively, and in a way peculiar to the people of Shavi, all eyes turned, not to Asogba, not to Egbongbele, but to the angry priest, Anoku. He had been debating what to do. If he went on ranting like the last time, people wouldn't listen to him, for in Shavi, dignity commands more respect than position. If he lost his dignity, he would lose his credibility. He was the priest, chosen by his father who was also a priest. But if he insisted on foretelling doom or warning the king and the people of Shavi about what they didn't want to hear, he suspected that the new radical young prince would remove him. He could justify it by saying that the voice of the people of Shavi is the voice of Ogene. People of Shavi were like that. Live and let live. And if they removed him, his position and the position of his beloved daughter, Ayoko, would be at stake.

His mind went back to the day Ayoko was born. He knew that Ayoko's mother, being a young woman, would have more children later, and the first son would be a priest after him. But how was he sure that Ayoko's mother would have a son, or that he, Anoku, would ever have a son? So, not wanting to be like the man who poured away the water he had in his water pot simply because he heard the sounds of thunder, Anoku had run to the Ogene lake and started to pray loudly. Most people in Shavi had seen him praying, and had said that whilst his wife laboured for Ayoko, he was asking Ogene what her future held. Eventually he heard a woman shouting, "It's a girl, it's a girl!" Anoku heard the woman, got up and took another track into the palace, where he told King Patayon that Ogene had just told him that the daughter of the priest would be the future Queen Mother.

"Congratulations," King Patayon had said. "I don't see why not, if my son Asogba, who is now eight years old, can wait for her to grow up."

"It is the command, my king" Anoku had insisted. "And don't congratulate me. I don't know whether my wife has given birth or not. I went to the Ogene lake to pray and make sacrifice because I was summoned to do so. The women are with my wife, but Ogene told me through prayers that the future queen of Shavi is being born, and I ran to tell you, my king."

"Then if your wife has a boy, we will . . . "

"Ogene does not lie, my king."

"Yes, of course," King Patayon had said quickly. "You must forgive my inattention.

The priest went into a trance, from which Shoshovi and many women in the palace tried to talk him out and get him to eat, but he kept mumbling and intoning. After a while, he motioned to those around him to go to his house and check whether his wife had given birth or not. The messenger came to the palace of King Patayon and said in the presence of all assembled that Anoku's young wife had given birth to a woman child.

"Not to a woman child, but to the greatest Queen Mother Shavi will ever see," Anoku declared, coming out of his trance. This incident enhanced his reputation a great deal. Ayoko was betrothed to Asogba right from the day she was born. Anoku now had sons as well, so his grip was strong on Shavi. All this he didn't want to lose because of some leper-looking people who looked as slimy and nauseating as worms.

Having arrived at this conclusion, whilst all eyes were still on him he raised his hand to indicate to Asogba that he was free to say whatever he wanted to say. After all, it is very unwise to cut down the tree that bears the fruit. Asogba was going to be his son-in-law, and King soon. So it would be unwise to encourage Ogene to predict anything against him.

"Thank you, he who speaks the language of the birds. A thought just occurred to me. Do you realise what advantage it would be to us if we could fly? We could extend the borders of Shavi to take in Bordue, and Afli, our troublesome neighbours. Wait until they see us fly, then they will respect our Ogene and not the Mohammed they wail to day and night.''

"The funniest thing is that they look down on us for worshipping Ogene. They call us Kaferi, infidels. Now we'll be able to show them how great Ogene is,'' Mensa said.

"We have until now been swallowing their insults, but not any more. Not since we made friends with these leper people. They will tell us all their secrets. Our neighbours will hear from us by and by,'' Asogba went on enthusiastically.

Patayon looked long at his son and shook his head, whilst his face wore a bland, vacant smile. Then he asked, "How are they going to hear from us?''

"We'll descend on them. We'll let them know who is the boss in this place and if they refuse to accept it, we'll make war on them. It would be exciting to show our neighbours what we're capable of achieving.''

"War, war, war,'' Egbongbele drawled, in a slow, tired voice. "Wars are costly of human lives. We have never made wars on our neighbours because we didn't possess great birds to show off. Now we have great birds to show off, we talk of wars. That isn't progress.''

"But wise one, all our neighbours make wars on each other. They leave us be, but some of them think we're cowards. Now they'll learn that the people of Shavi are strong,'' Asogba went on, warming to his subject.

"I like to watch youthful enthusiasm, it can be so infectious. Our neighbours let us be because we spend our time producing enough food for our people, and making each other happy, simply by sharing our problems. All these may not be glamorous to the youth, but believe me, Asogba, our great great grandparents trod all those miles between us and the Kokumas to achieve these things. So they must be worth preserving, don't you think, my son?''

''My father, the king, as you said, those things happened a long, long time ago. Even your grandfather couldn't remember it, but had to be told the story. We're now the children of today. Ogene in her goodness has sent us people to tell us what is happening in far-off places. I'm sure there are places farther than Ongar, Blimer and our cattle market. If we lose this opportunity, father, how do we know that she won't send them to our neighbours, the Mohammed worshippers?''

Egbongbele looked at his friend of many years, and they both smiled knowingly. The latter said, ''The sun is getting hotter and here we are talking like a silly man who wants his son to run before he can walk. We haven't even been able to talk to our new friends yet. We're not even sure they'll be willing to part with their secrets. But what we are sure of is this, their chief has sunken eyes like someone who can think. So we should introduce him to our cows, let him stay with them in the valley of the cow-herds and indulge his thinking habits.''

''Don't you think, father, that he should be allowed to sit in the palace compound with us and talk sometimes?'' Asogba persisted.

''Asogba, Asogba, don't forget you're a prince. You should uphold the laws of the land. Let the most intelligent looking among them go and look after the cows. If he succeeds in herding the animals, then we'll see whether he can sit with us men. Meanwhile, encourage the women to teach him our language,'' Anoku said, looking from one face to the other as if expecting an accolade.

Mensa started to laugh at his obvious behaviour. All eyes shifted from Anoku to him.

''I'm sorry,'' he said quickly. ''I wasn't laughing at our priest, but I do find it funny to note that our prince wants to learn the secrets of a people whose chief we think is fit only to be company to our cows.''

''Our cows are perfectly intelligent animals!'' Anoku said, suppressing a dry smile.

''Egbongbele ignored Mensa and Anoku and went on talking as if addressing Asogba alone. ''We are cattle people. Our cows are our life, our money and our livelihood. What greater honour can we give a new person than for him to be asked to help us in looking after our cattle?'' He turned slowly to Mensa. ''We are cattle people, people who think and don't speak if they have nothing to say.''

The stupid grin vanished from Mensa's face.

7

Shavi Crystals

It was still dark outside when Flip and Ronje walked into their thatched dome house. Flip silently gestured to Ronje not to talk as the gentle breathing of the others could still be heard.

"I know," said Ronje, nodding vigorously and lowering his voice to a whisper. "This is the best part of the day in this Godforsaken place."

Flip grinned wickedly. "They didn't invite us, remember. We gate crashed into Shavi and are now disturbing their way of life."

"Their way of life! People's way of life! Don't make me laugh, Flip. These aren't people, they're rootless savages. See, our shower is only a calabash of water."

"You can go to the lake if you want a complete bath. Nobody is forcing you not to, Ronje," Flip said dryly.

"And be mobbed by those gaping children. I'm sure they've never seen a human being before, the way they look at us." Ronje started to smile to himself, as if recollecting an amusing incident. He dipped his chin into his chest, forming fleshy creases around his neck, like the heavy neck beads worn by some of the women of Shavi. Then he shot his round chin up and looked, self-confidently at Flip. "That serving girl is deeper than you think. She makes love with her eyes. One shouldn't be concerned though. I'm sure she's only a slave or something like that, sent purposely to entertain us. Poor girl, hm . . . None of us has taken advantage of what is offered us on a plate.''

Flip gestured Ronje to the little corner reserved for washing. They both washed themseleves in silence, and afterwards Flip started to comb his hair with the wooden comb they had been given. He looked through the narrow gap in the round house and remarked absentmindedly as if Ronje hadn't spoken at all. "People seem to be up early this morning. It looks as if something's going to happen today.''

"They're probably going to cook and eat us all, one by one.''

"Ronje, you seem to be under pressure. But so are we all. If it means anything to you, I'm going to the place of the crash to see whether we can make anything of the remains of the Newark. Would you like to join me?''

Ronje hesitated, but looked through the gap with Flip. A mixture of anger and frustration seemed to have completely enveloped him. "I believed you once," he cried. "You built this marvellous machine, one that would never crash, that could stay days in the air, that would never burn or burst into flames, that would protect us from radiation effects by its lead shielding. And what happened? It crashed within hours. It burst into flames . . . ''

"But it didn't burn. At least, it didn't burn itself to cinders,'' Flip interjected.

"It didn't burn! Ha! Do you hear that? It didn't burn!'' Ronje's voice rose. It dawned then on Flip watching him that he had triggered off words that had to be spoken. He wisely kept quiet and let the torrent of reproaches flow. But when it seemed that Ronje would never stop, Flip became concerned for his friend and colleague.

"For heaven's sake, Ronje, collect yourself and stop ranting. You can't even have a quiet morning sleep in this place. It's impossible to sleep at night, because of the damned heat.

Now I want to sleep in the morning, what do I get, what do I get . . . Ronje ranting like a madman,'' Mendoza complained, as he turned his face to the wall and snuggled deeper into his sleeping sheet.

"Are you fighting with Ronje, Flip?" Kisskiss's voice piped up from the other side of the thatched one-room house.

"No, Kisskiss darling, they're having a nice civilised little talk, the only way they know how to," Ista supplied.

"I'm sorry, everybody," Flip began but was stopped as Ronje gave him an unexpected blow on the side of his cheek.

"Sorry? Sorry? Haven't you made enough havoc? Moshem is gone. Tara is gone. Kisskiss almost died . . .''

"Stop it, stop it, the two of you!" Andria screamed from her corner.

"I think Ronje's going mad," Mendoza grumbled sleepily.

"He's right in a way. The first Noah saved his people. I didn't. I crashed into this place, but what I was suggesting was that we should find a way of going back. We can't stay here for the rest of our lives. If the button hasn't been pressed, as we feared, I don't see why we shouldn't go back."

"Why can't you allow yourself to be angry like everybody else, Flip? Many mortals can't stand perfect people. The crash, the death of Moshem and Tara . . . Were they just your fault? Were you forced to join the Newark flying club, Ronje? Or are you just angry because Flip didn't share your enthusiasm about the serving girl?" Ista asked, getting up.

The laughter that greeted this remark was unreal, humourless. It emanated from Mendoza, who stood there by a dark curve of the one-roomed house. He presented a magnificent, if ghostly picture, in the white body cloth given to him by the Queen Mother, with his bare feet, and his matted head thrown back in vacant amusement. Mendoza's laughter went on and on, like a canned laughter machine. As he exhausted himself, the laughter diluted into giggles. It was upsetting to Dorf, who thought the world of his father.

"What's wrong, daddy?" Dorf asked.

The silence that followed this childish question was more moving than the cry of a widow who has just lost a rare and friendly husband. The adults looked at each other guiltily. As it looked as if the silence was going to be prolonged, Andria pointed at Ronje and asked, "Why do you wear such ridiculous underpants in the mornings?"

"I jog in the mornings, remember? I jog for my sanity and for my physical health. Or maybe I have to ask for permission from your Flip to even do that?"

"No, Ronje, you don't need permission to jog," Andria said, smiling in a conciliatory way.

Andria's teasing remark, followed by her equitable reply, helped to dispel the tension that was building among the members of the Newark club.

No one had suggested Ronje should apologise to Flip for hitting him on the side of his jaw. He knew that people felt he could take it, but whether they felt he deserved it or not, was something he still couldn't make out. He rubbed the painful side of his mouth, staring piercingly at his attacker, hoping for an apology. But Flip didn't get one. He got the point. He knew now from the silent stares of his friends that Ronje was speaking the thoughts of them all and that Mendoza's laughter had expressed their feelings, whether towards him, Ronje, or their ludicrous situation, was not quite clear.

Flip's gaze softened as it rested on Andria. She was in the same kind of body cloth that swathed the rest of the group. She draped hers so artlessly that, though it covered most of her body, the tail end of it swept the floor. It made her look like a huge, white fish. Flip searched her eyes for some sympathy, but they were resolutely turned away from him.

He must get these people away from here. Whatever befell them after that would be their own problem.

He turned abruptly, walked away from the group, and dressed

himself rapidly. The atmosphere in the vaulted room was becoming stifling. The people of Shavi had been kind to them in the only way they knew how. They had given them the best house in town, coming second only to their King's palace in beauty and size. The visitors had spent their first few days shouting, demonstrating and gesticulating in English, French and German, but the Shavians had simply smiled in their polite way and shaken their heads negoatively. They didn't understand them. A thought occurred to Flip at this stage: that they must have sounded barbaric to these gentle people. Then that nice middle-aged woman, who seemed to command respect, and a group of young women, had started to take care of them. But they knew that somehow they were being watched, if not as potential enemies, then as curiosities, by the boyish-looking soldiers and guards. And apart from the word, "mesiere", which they said to them when coming in and going out, none of them said much at all. They would announce their presence by clapping four times, then simply glide in, their body cloth covering even their ankles. They would do their jobs, then glide out again, repeating "mesiere".

Flip took a smaller piece of cloth, tied it round his head, and walked out towards the place of the crash. He didn't say a word to any of his friends.

The sun was already getting hot and, though the sand was quite thick and comparatively cool, he knew that soon it would be burning his flesh. He had to make a thorough inspection of the plane, and he had to make it quickly before the heat became unbearable.

He walked round the Newark. He had been right: parts of the plane had started to smoke on impact with the ground, but it hadn't actually burnt. They had lost some valuable equipment, otherwise the body of the Newark was still intact. Why was Ronje saying what he was saying? Simply to spike his guns?

He was for a while tempted to be sorry for himself. Maybe they ought not to have left. He knew he was one of those unorthodox scientists, who believed in God. When he told his colleagues of his beliefs, they had dubbed him a dreamer. Maybe they were right, maybe he had simply wanted to find out how long they could survive in the Newark. Was that why he'd been so keen on the escapade? But he'd been sure that the Western civilised world would blow itself up. Now here they were, among a people wallowing and growing fat in their apparent ignorance. Flip wished they could hurry away and leave these people to their contented way of life.

Just look at how Andria had behaved a week or so ago! When they crashed into Shavi, Kisskiss had had such a bad shock that even Ista thought she wouldn't survive and feared that if no medical attention was given, it could affect her brain. Andria had been so shocked herself that she went into a near coma for days. When she came round days later, she screamed at the middle aged Shavi woman who was rubbing oil over Kisskiss and saying soothing words, like the humming of overfed bees on a lazy hot afternoon. "Leave my daughter alone, you . . ." Andria had shouted as soon as her eyes were open.

"Don't say that, Andria, she's been looking after Kisskiss since you've been too ill to take care of her," Flip had said.

Andria could hardly control herself. But as soon as Shoshovi left the room, she made it clear that she didn't want the woman cooing over Kisskiss and rubbing that smelly stuff on her. Thank goodness Kisskiss solved the problem herself by starting to walk and talk normally. They were all still watching for the brain damage which Ista had warned could take place. Nonetheless, Flip knew that Andria wouldn't be able to rest until she had had Kisskiss properly examined in a hospital.

He kicked a piece of stone in anger. "But what is happening out there, in the rest of the world? Which way should one walk

55

or fly to get away from this place? The people of Shavi from all appearances were not affected by whatever was happening elsewhere. They had a few cows per family, and seldom travelled more than a few miles from their community. Nothing seemed to have happened, despite the nuclear blast, which meant that their world was still there, so they must go back. The only problem was how? How was he to raise the plane into the air now that the engine had been partly destroyed? Perhaps he could rebuild it, but what about the leakage in the fuel tank? By now, all the fuel would have leaked into the mud. A scanty patch of bush separated the Shavian city wall from where the Newark had crashed, but otherwise it was all rocky earth. Flip wondered how anything managed to grow and survive in a place like this. He could understand the few trees, clustering around the lakes in the centre of the town, but away from the lakes, one's nostrils were assaulted by an arid dryness. They had been here for fourteen days now, and though it had threatened to rain many times, what actually fell was not even enough to saturate the thick sand. Yet, in between the tiny rocks, some plants survived. Flip got temporarily carried away, almost forgetting that he had left the house in order to examine the Newark. Like a little boy on an urgent errand, side-tracked by a bird's nest, Flip walked towards a pile of rocks, to discover, between the knuckles of rock, cacti shrubs bearing tiny pinky-yellow flowers. These flowers had strong prickly petals. Flip touched them. "I wonder how you get your pollination, by your attraction? Surely no bee could survive after touching you? He plucked one of the flowers and was surprised to see what at first looked like a tiny, shiny bird's egg. But it was not an egg, it was a stone. He threw it on the ground, but it didn't chip. It looked like a piece of polished crystal – like a diamond. Could diamonds be found so near the surface of the earth? This was definitely not an ordinary stone. He went deeper into the rocks, walking towards the big lake and found that, hidden from view, were many of these curious-looking flowers. Then he noticed the place was full of creatures like huge spiders, or perhaps scorpions. As they heard the sound of his footsteps, he could see that they began to dart from one side of the rocks to the other. Gingerly he collected three more of the stones and started to make his way from the shadows of the rocks towards the open.

How could a stone this tough be found so near the surface? Flip looked upwards and could see the gentle rise of the hills surrounding Shavi. Were these hills volcanic, and did they throw up valuable stones from the womb of the earth? Were there more of them? He must come back and study them much more closely. But meanwhile he must be quiet about it, he didn't want to build up anybody's hopes unnecessarily.

He made his way back. He had scarcely reached the footpath that led to the place where the Newark rested before he heard the voices of men from the palace. They started to call, "Onye isi, onye isi!" Flip turned and smiled.

The two young men smiled too and pointed to Asogba, who was standing a little way off, carrying what looked like a spear and stick.

Flip was taken aback. Since they had arrived, they had never been called for anything. The young men carrying the spears had always been polite and smiling. For once, a little fear crept into his mind concerning their safety. The two men led him to Asogba. As Flip reached him, he embraced him, still smiling, and he and the other men began to laugh. Flip, not knowing what to do, started to laugh with them. At least laughter was a universal language. He might as well join in.

Then suddenly Asogba stopped laughing and began to talk rapidly to the other men. He pointed at himself and said, "Asogba," very, very slowly, repeating it several times, so that Flip got the idea. He nodded his head and said, "Introduction time, eh?" After fourteen days?" He pointed at himself and said "Flip," and they all laughed again.

Flip was led back to their house, to be fed with the usual delicious maizy stuff which they always had for breakfast. He
could tell that it was sweetened with honey and that it was
milky. They all loved it, and Kisskiss had given it the name
"white custard".

Mendoza, who was eating when Flip entered with Asogba
and the guards, pretended not to see him. Then he looked up
suddenly and exclaimed artificially, "Ah, we were wondering
what they had done to you. You're right, we must find a way
of leaving this place. They're urging us to eat and we don't
know for what."

"They always give us breakfast, though," Ista said.

"Yes, but this is different. There's an air of excitement.
You don't need to understand their language to know that
they're up to something. Maybe they're going to start killing
us, one by one. We wouldn't be missed. Nobody knows
where we are. It would be easy for them to get away with it."

"Please stop saying things like that, John Mendoza, you
don't think of the children at all, do you? Why can't you just
accept kindness without reading some ill meaning into it?
People are sometimes just kind to each other, you know," Flip
protested.

"They'd be inhuman to want to kill us and still be this
happy and excited, " Ista persisted, looking thoughtful.

"Wouldn't you be excited and happy if you were promised
a nice steak dinner?" Mendoza asked.

"No, I don't like meat," Ista spat.

"I don't like meat, either," Dorf declared flatly.

"Me too!" Kisskiss piped, with her mouth full of "white
custard".

"There you are, nobody believes you," Andria put in.
"Kisskiss and Dorf have made friends with the children of
Shavi, haven't you?"

"We went fishing and nut cracking yesterday. It was hot though," Dorf said.

They went on spooning the porridge into their mouths.

Though they didn't talk about their doubts, they were all worried and jumpy. They stopped eating automatically when Asogba came in in his usual way, by clapping his hands four times in the doorway.

He smiled again and told the others his name in the same way he had to Flip.

"You'd better tell him your names because I have. I think they want to get to know us better from now on."

"I know, I know, father, they're not going to kill us. I think they want us to be their friends. You don't kill things whose names you know, do you, father?"

"Yeah, yeah," Kisskiss piped so high that Asogba laughed and started to call Kisskiss "Yeah, yeah," thinking that was her name.

However, when Flip had to go out with Asogba, he said gravely, "He's been wanting to lead me somewhere, I don't know where. And I've never seen him carrying this staff before. But if I don't come back with them, find a way to escape from here".

"Oh, for God's sake, Flip stop talking like that! I'm sure they're just going to show you something," Andria cried, clinging to him. It was during this time that Flip slipped the four stones he was carrying in his trousers into her hand, at the same time pressing her for silence. The urgency of the situation flowed from Flip to Andria. She clutched at the stones, not daring to look at them, for she could feel Ronje's eyes boring into her back. She bit her lip and took a hold of herself. Something told her that Flip would return safely, but how could she be quite sure?

"My gun still works, Flip," Ronje said unexpectedly.

"No, keep it out of sight, and don't be a fool. You may need it.'' With that, Flip followed Asogba from the narrow door into the open courtyard.

Surprised and bemused, they all watched as one of the women brought out a head cover for Flip, pointing to the sun as she did so. This made Flip shout to his friends, ''She's saying that it's going to be very hot and I need to have my head covered.''

This brought a temporary smile of relief to the faces of the frightened visitors. The smile became broader when one of the men, who seemed now to be only attendants, gave the same kind of staff that Asogba was carrying to Flip.

''At least he can defend himself with that if need be,'' Ronje said under his breath.

''I know our problem; we simply find it difficult to accept kindness,'' Ista declared, looking unexpectedly happy.

As Flip left, though he didn't know where they were going, and despite all the doubts, he felt he could trust the humanity of the people of Shavi. They had not acquired the art of superficial kindness. Their kindness was humane and genuine. So Flip tied his head cloth more securely, held his desert walking stick firmly, and followed Asogba and his men.

8
False Alarm

When Asogba, Flip and the young staff and package carriers left the compound, a kind of emptiness descended on the rest of the crew of the Newark. If only they could understand the Shavian language, if only they could communicate to them what all the excitement was about. Were they happy because, as Ronje had hinted, they were probably going to have them all for a feast tonight? They all knew that Ronje could be over-dramatic, but the thought of what he had said lingered.

Andria felt too weary to do anything. She couldn't even think. It was getting hot already and that would knock her out for the greater part of the day. She heard Ronje say that they should take Flip's advice and see what could be done with the wreck of the Newark. "At least we can find out where we are," Andria sighed with resignation.

Mendoza suddenly took hold of his head and started to shake it from side to side. Ista watched him closely, remembering that he had had a nasty knock when they crash landed. "You have to mind that head, you know. You shouldn't be shaking it like that," she warned.

Mendoza laughed one of his joyless laughs. "I'll try not to think too much, doctor. I may be losing it tonight anyway."

Andria looked around her desperately and urged the children to go and join the Shavian children, whose voices could be heard outside. Dorf obediently took Kisskiss's hand and went out.

Soon their own laughter joined with that of the Shavian children. "I don't understand children. They don't seem to care at all," Andria said.

"Maybe because there's nothing to worry about," Ista said, optimistically.

Andria sat down on the cool floor with her legs wide apart to let in air, and tucked her waist cloth between her legs, the way she had seen the women of Shavi do. Her thoughts strayed back to Flip. She would ask him to marry her if he ever returned alive from wherever these strange people had taken him. She knew that Flip, like Dorf and Kisskiss, trusted them. The only weak trait in Flip was that he was too trusting. She remembered the day they had met. She was one of the hundreds of women blocking the way to the Nuclear Research Institute where he worked. Kisskiss was then only three years old, and it was cold. Flip singled her out and came to her where she was queueing for a mug of soup for Kisskiss. He had pretended to be one of the protestors. He had said, "Don't you think you should take that child home and warm her, rather than let her die of cold here?"

"She won't have a future if I don't bring her here to protest against the decision of our president. It's mad to spend all that money on nuclear energy."

"I agree with you, but the thing is, it may never happen, and this child will be in danger if she stays here another day. Have you no one to take care of her?"

Andria had told him that even if she had had someone, she would not have sent Kisskiss to them. This encounter with a determined mother prepared to risk her child had made Flip rethink his position. It was only much later than Andria knew that Flip was the great professor, Philip Wagner. He had tried to halt the course of history from within the Institute, but when he knew that he was helpless, had devised this curiously-shaped glider with the help of Moshem, Ronje, Ista and the others. They had sold almost all they had, and, like many people, fled, when they suspected that their world was going to be destroyed. It now appeared as if they had been misled, but there had been nothing left for them to do at the time. Few people were willing to take such a chance, not knowing where they were going to land. Now see where it had landed them – among a people who didn't know what the other parts of the world were talking about. "If Flip lives, we must get back," she said with determination.

"Funny, we should be thinking the same thoughts," Ista answered from the cooler side of their vaulted home.

"Suppose they've blown the world up?"

"Heh, this is still part of the world, you know. We would have felt it, even here."

"But Ista, where is this? It's a desert, but which desert?"

"I think we must be somewhere in Africa. Judging from what we've seen, the people are content, work hard and enjoy it . . . ."

Just as if they had heard what she was saying, three women came in with Ayoko. They gave the two gaping white women long grasses tied together for sweeping. Amid a lot of giggles, they tied a head cloth on Andria and Ista and showed them how to sweep.

"I think I'm beginning to guess. We're being turned into white slaves," Andria said between clenched teeth.

"An alarmist like Ronje, aren't you? I think they simply want us to be part of them. I don't mind. I lived and worked for over five years in Burma, and before I could pick up a single Burmese word, I had to trust the humanity of the people. And mostly as a result of this, I got kindness in return all the way."

"But these people look so simple and silly to me."

"Why, because they smile a lot? Would they look more intelligent to you if they sat about glumly?"

"Oh Ista, you know what I mean. I don't like to see a group

of people in picturesque ignorance, however romantic it seems.''

''I really don't think I know what you mean. Look at us. We ran away from our over-civilised society because we were about to destroy ourselves. We landed here among people who haven't got the faintest idea about the bomb, who are perfectly happy and sure enough of themselves to trust and welcome us into their midst . . . If all this is stupidity, please God, or Allah, or whatever you're called, give it to me!''

The high laughter of the Shavi women interrupted this dialogue. They thought Ista and Andria looked funny in the off-white house cloths they had tied around them, and as for the head cloths, they kept slipping from their silky hair, and had to be tied and retied to get them to stay.

Andria looked at Ista, who seemed to be enjoying it all, and had to smile. That a trained medical mind like Ista's could degenerate into this romantic, giggly woman, was something beyond her. She tried to recall the well-dressed doctor who was so sure of her subject, but could not.

She opened her hand to accept the long grass broom and realised that in her great tension she was still holding the crystals Flip had given her. As she stared at them frowning, Ista saw her and asked, ''What are those, earrings?''

''Yes,'' Andria replied quickly. She dashed back into the house, indicating by gesticulation to the standing women that she would not be long.

It was dark inside their vaulted house. And with everybody out, the circular interior was a strong contrast to the bright dusty outside. Andria opened her hands again and felt the smoothness of the pieces. They were shaped like eggs, though they were too tiny. Andria decided that they were more like seeds. But seeds of what? Where had Flip got them from? What were they? She was not a woman who wore diamonds, and couldn't tell the real from the fake anyway. The nearest

she had got to wearing expensive jewels was the ring which
Flip had bought her, when they had decided that their friend-
ship was above marriage, as a mark of their unique relationship. She had given him a gold chain, which he still wore. She
couldn't tell what these were, but of one thing she was sure,
they couldn't be diamonds, for don't people dig for diamonds?

"Andria, Andria, come out of hiding, will you?"

"Shan't be long, Ista," Andria called back, surprised at herself. She took out one of Kisskiss's dresses, tied the crystals up
in it and placed them under the child's straw pillow. Then she
came out into the glare, and followed the other women into
the palace compound.

The day turned out to be a really happy one. The Shavian
women taught Ista and Andria the words for food, child,
broom, wood and men. They all laughed a great deal. The dust
was disturbing, because the more they swept the more it rose,
floating around before settling down again. Then when the
sun was at its highest, they had a delicious meal of fish and
fruits and drank what Ista said was barley beer. They only discovered the alcoholic content of this drink much later.

They were led to another part of the huge compound where
another group of women were laughing and singing, and to
their astonishment, Ista and Andria started to laugh and sing
with them. At the end of the first song, most of the women left
what they were doing, and walked up to Ista and Andria with
arms wide open in welcome and embraced them with warmth.

"Well, take that look of fear and mistrust off your face,
Andria. We're being taught the universal lingo – laughter,
happiness and food."

"And alcohol," Andria declared with a hiccough.

"Do you think we're drunk?" Ista asked.

Andria started to laugh recklessly. "Oh Ista, you're the
doctor, you should know. But I suspect that that drink you
call barley beer has more alcohol than any whisky."

"Alarmist!"

"You always say that!"

Nobody brought them water for baths that day, but they were able to guess that they had either to fetch the water for themselves or go to one of the lakes and wash. Ista and Andria preferred the latter option. By the time they got to their house, they were deliciously tired and refreshed. They were met by Mendoza who didn't look too unhappy either.

"Where's Flip, is he back?" Andria couldn't hide the agitation in her voice, despite the alcohol.

"Alright, alright, there he is, flat on his back, our great scientist, drunk as a lord," Mendoza pointed, shaking his head knowingly.

Flip was lying on his back as usual with little on. The straw fan he always carried in Shavi was lying on his chest. His breath rose and fell like a child's. One hand was over his head, and the other lay by his side. He was sleeping a sleep of satisfaction and contentment. The people of Shavi had not killed Flip. They had no intention of killing any of them. How could they? Did they themselves not run away from killers in the land of the Kokumas? But the white invaders didn't know this, didn't even suspect it. They thought that they had escaped from a nuclear holocaust only to be plunged into a savage society. But these "savages" happened to be noble people who never forgot their past history.

Andria stared at Flip long and hard. Flip opened his eyes, and was instantly awake. "We've been made citizens of Shavi," Flip announced with a wide yawn and an equally huge stretch of his arms.

"Was that the reason for the celebration?" Ista asked from the hammock in which she was swinging in another corner.

"That, and also the chief or the king – I can't make out which he is really – is getting himself a new wife tonight."

"I say, Flip. How did you know all that?" Ronje enquired.

Flip got up, exaggerating his yawn to tell Ronje that he was asking a stupid question which didn't need an answer.

It had all been a false alarm. The albino people would have to learn to accept kindness without strings. It would take them a long time because life was so seldom like that in the society from which they came. But for the people of Shavi, during the time when the albinos were still new among them, this was the only way they knew for one human to behave towards another.

9
The Dancing Queen

The moon was shining very brightly this night. The sand and the little rocks all took the moon's silvery colour. It was getting cool, almost cold, and the dust of the day now rested around the cacti shrubs and among the egbos. The night sound of insects, bush monkeys and owls, with the occasional unearthly laughter of hyenas, took over from the day noises of domesticated animals – the cows, the fowls and the goats.

Inside the circular house, dim light from the wooden candle holder gave a limpid illumination. The light gave off an oily smell which was not offensive and which mixed with the fragrance of the spicy barley dough they were eating. The light fishy soup was rather less in quantity than usual, and Ronje had remarked, ''Maybe they're going to start starving us''.

''Starving you for what?'' Flip asked, chewing his food in meditative amusement.

''So that we won't be able to fight back.''

Ista laughed and replied, ''You always look for the worst traits in others, don't you Ronje? I can tell you were badly hurt as a child.''

''If you don't trust easily, then you don't get hurt,'' responded Ronje, smacking his lips noisily, as if to press home his point.

''Oh yes, talking of trust, did you manage to do anything on the Newark, or did our hosts take you to their cow farm too?''

Flip asked, partly to change the subject and partly to humour Ronje.

"Cow farm, cow farm? Was that where you went, Flip? But whatever for? Do they think you're a cow-herd?"

Flip, with his brows raised, holding a drinking calabash in the air, actually looked the part of a desert cow-herd, provoking general laughter. Mendoza laughed the loudest, his rich tenor voice ringing out as if he was singing.

In that instant, the Newark crew in the badly-lit room in the middle of the desert knew that, if they were going to be in any danger, it was going to be the danger they would bring upon themselves. The people of Shavi didn't plan to harm them.

"There was a kind of counting going on," Flip began to explain. "We persuaded the cows to go this way, so that they could be counted, and sixty-five huge beasts were then driven into the interior. We eventually chose ten. And what a deal of grooming and cleaning the poor animals had."

"And, Professor Wagner, were you good at it, I mean, grooming and cleaning cows?" Mendoza asked.

"You mean you were bullied into cleaning cows with savages? What an honour," Ronje added.

"But just listen, how were these people to know that Flip's an eminent and respected scientist? To them, maybe because of his red beard, he's fit only to look after cows. We had to cook and to eat with our fingers, and drink barley beer, which I thoroughly enjoyed," Ista went on.

"And I was drunk," Andria interjected, with a theatrical guffaw.

"You never think of the danger," Ronje said. "Viruses and all that."

"Well, put it this way, Ronje, I jogged three times a week, I ate the right fibre, I dieted and all for what? So that I wouldn't die of cancer or obesity, but only fourteen days ago, we were almost dead. Some of us did die."

"Oh Ista, it's been a happy day. Don't please," Andria implored.

There was a clapping of hands at the door, accompanied by the light happy laughter of young girls.

Involuntarily, Ronje got up and said under his breath, "It's that little servant's teasing laughter. I can tell her voice anywhere". The others watched him as he made for the door. He peered outside and was confronted with the moon's silvery brightness, the graceful indistinct shadows of the egbos, and very near him four girls, wrapped in what looked like plain dazzling sheets, giggling at him.

As they saw him, Ayoko whispered something to the others, and laughed even louder. The laughter was so transparently innocent that Ronje for once forgot his moodiness and smiled. He saw before him straight perfected creatures, clean and uncomplicated as rain. He could guess their slimness even though they were all wrapped in loose white body cloths. Their dark hair was partly covered, and along their brows were colourful strings of beads. They were wearing sandals on their feet, and these too had beads on them. In their bare arms lay folded cloths that had evidently been washed, laundered and made ready to be worn. Ayoko gestured to him that the body cloths were for them. She used her free hand to show him how they were to be worn.

"Alright, alright. I get your point. I may not understand a word of what you say, but I'm not daft. But what's the celebration for, huh? What's all this hullaballoo about? Are you going to dress us up, then cook and eat us?"

"For God's sake, old chap." Flip walked towards the door to take the body cloths from the girls. "Thank you, mesiere," he said gravely.

Ayoko and the waiting girls said, "Thank you, mesiere," as well. They found it all very funny when they realised that they too were learning to speak the language of the albino people.

Flip took the cloths in and said, "I think they want us to put these on. There's a kind of celebration tonight. That was probably why we had to bring those cows from the fields."

"Where do the cows graze?" Ista asked.

"We walked for over three hours in what looked like a southerly direction. I only had the sun to guide me."

"Well, I'm glad to know that your knowledge of science is being of some use."

"Look, Ronje, you weren't forced into this project. If things go wrong, why can't you just accept it? Now, we've rested, we should try to communicate with the rest of the world. This is an isolated place, hidden from view by the surrounding desert and hills. I'm sure that if we took a compass and climbed one of those hills I saw this afternoon, we should be able to tell where we were."

"I know we're not in the Antarctic, or the North Pole," Dorf, who had been listening to the adults, interjected.

Flip smiled at him and ran an indulgent hand over his head. "What are you going to be when you grow up, Dorf?" Flip asked playfully.

"Astronomer," came the prompt reply.

"I wanted to be an astronomer first." Kisskiss wouldn't be left out.

As the group started to laugh, the girls at the door clapped. They came in and urged the visitors to dress.

The coolness of the night struck the albino visitors as they came out of their house. On first arriving in Shavi, you might think it was an arid land, for the lands around the main village were so flat that at first the white visitors thought they were in a complete desert. But this was not so. The early settlers had walked through a gap between two hills, made up of deceptively dry, loose rocks. They didn't know that the mountains were volcanic, and could be active again. Shavi had marvelled at the perfection of the land he found and was surprised to know

71

years later that their nearest neighbours were about ten trek-king days away. These long distances could be made a little shorter by using donkeys. The people of Shavi were quite satis-fied with their lives. They visited their neighbours sometimes, simply to exchange news, and to buy camels and other items made from camelskin. Once in a while, they would display their animals, just to show their might, so they wouldn't be attacked. They were never frightened of invaders, since their mountain and desert surroundings offered them adequate pro-tection against enemies.

During the day, the desert air was hot and dry, at night cool to the point of coldness, as now. The white visitors walked slowly in their new Shavi sandals, feeling conspicuous. They enjoyed the smoothness of the hand-woven body cloth they had been given.

Ayoko and the other girls were delighted to see them so well dressed. They all walked slowly and gracefully towards the palace walls, forgetting the danger they had felt earlier in the day, except for Ronje, who could trust no one, and had his gun fully loaded in the shorts he wore under the cloth. Flip could think what he liked, but he wasn't going to trust his life to these strange people.

Then they heard fine music coming from within the palace walls. Many male voices were singing in drawn-out haunting voices, reminiscent of religious chanting. No drums were being beaten, but they heard stringed instruments like guitars. One got used to the regularity after a while, but their sounds touched the sensitivity in such a mysterious way that they felt they could listen to them for ever.

"I think I can guess what that instrument is," Flip volun-teered before they saw the musicians, who were hidden on one side of the palace walls.

"Whatever it is, its poignancy is haunting. I've never heard anything so fine before," Ista observed.

"I think they're playing their own version of the kora."

"But kora is played singly, by one person only. These are many voices, and many of them are playing the same . . . yes . . . it's kora," Ronje reluctantly agreed.

"Then I think I can guess where we are. It has to be Africa. No other place in the world do you get people playing kora," Andria said with a note of relieved finality.

"Wee . . . ll," Flip began.

"There's no well about it. If we're in Africa, we must be near one of its great deserts – the Sahara or the Kalahari."

"Pity we can't ask the people themselves," laughed Mendoza.

Andria began to giggle like the Shavi girls. She stopped in her tracks.

"Glad to see you laugh," Flip remarked.

"I'm remembering our civilisation. To think these people have been living here, surrounded by their desert, going about their own business and completely unaware of the west so that they don't even know the name we give the deserts surrounding them."

"Oh no, Andria, oh no. If you're entertaining the idea of civilising the people of Shavi, I'm not going to let you. Just leave them be. We should try to find our way out and face our own problems. We must try to forget we ever met these people," Ista cried.

"You mean, leave them in their picturesque ignorance? How romantic!" said Ronje sarcastically.

"And what do you mean by that?" Ista snapped.

"I've seen that loosely built young man, the tall one with the lopsided grin and rickety legs, examining the Newark. He didn't take anything, but I couldn't help noticing the seriousness on his face. Behind his lopsided smile, I can sense ambition. You can't keep his like in ignorance, not for long," Ronje explained, blunting his earlier sarcasm.

"Oh my God, not again," Andria wailed.

"Yes, I know what you mean, Andria. We took Christianity to them in West Africa, then we encouraged them to sell their brothers and sisters, and we're now buying up all their mineral deposits," Ista muttered.

"Oh yes, Flip talking of minerals," Andria said brightly. She always did this whenever a conversation or argument was becoming too disturbing for her comfort. "You know those stones you found, what are they?"

The group stopped and looked at Flip and Andria. Confused, Andria started to apologise. There was a mistrustful silence among the group of white people who stood there all covered in white body cloths, challenging each other, gauging each other's strength. "I'm sorry," Andria said again.

"What minerals have you two discovered, eh?" asked Mendoza, leaning towards Andria with an ugly sardonic leer.

"Alright, John, calm down. We haven't discovered another King Solomon's mines. I just found a few stones, though I'm not sure they're of any value. I couldn't tell you this morning because of the rush for me to go to the grazing fields. They looked precious and rather polished, but what puzzles me is that they were found on the surface, rather than inside the earth.

"Maybe those innocent-looking hills are volcanic," Ronje observed coolly. "I wouldn't be surprised at all, with the mountains you said you saw this morning. Mind you, we can see the outline from here . . . But I don't know. Where exactly did you find them?"

Flip deliberately avoided answering Ronje. Luckily, there was no time to pursue the subject as their hosts were looking out for them and had seen them standing there, just outside the palace walls, talking. Ayoko came out and ushered them in. The kora singers went on singing a song of welcome specially composed for the Ark group. Ista and Andria were ushered to one side, where sat most of the women who had worked with them during the day. They smiled their welcome and, as Andria was about to sit next to Ista, a middle-aged woman shook her head at them. "No, not there," she was saying in Shavian. Another woman was gently directing Andria away from Ista. For a while, the two white women were frightened, especially as a slight argument rose, the middle-aged woman saying something to Andria and rocking her arms at the same time. The kora singers, who seemed to need complete silence for the appreciation of their music, stopped playing. All eyes turned to the women. Andria's voice was raised and she cried in English, "But I want to sit with my friend. Where are you taking me?"

The white men, who were seated away from the women, watched closely. Flip noted the fear in Andria's voice, and Ronje fingered his gun. Without communicating to one another, the white men called up all the reserves in their bodies, ready to spring to Andria's defence if anyone became unnecessarily violent. But all was soon settled.

Ista, who was trying to follow the Shavian women's gesticulations, said conspiratorially to Andria, "I think they want you to sit just over there. Why don't you do what they say? I think they're telling you that I'm not the only friend you have, that they too are your friends. These women worked and sang with us this afternoon, remember, just do what they say".

"Maybe I'm going to be killed, as Ronje suggested," Andria thought wildly, but she steeled her nerves, did what Ista had said, and sat down next to the friendly woman. This gesture was greeted with clapping which the Ark group had learnt to associate with a sense of joyous approval.

"Oh, I see, they want us to be fully accepted. We put most visitors to our country in ghettos, but these people want us to mix with them. I wish I could speak their beautiful language," Flip said.

"I must say, you're right Flip. Its sibilance is thinly musical to the ear. And I've also noticed that there are no cripples or mongols, in fact no deformity," Mendoz observed.

"Now you mention it, so have I. Maybe it's the ideal temperature which produces everything in perfection."

But the people of Shavi did not, of course, have everything in perfection. Part of the celebration this night was to mark the end of a bitter and prolonged drought in which many people had died. They had no mongols or deformed people, because they got rid of them at birth, and those that lived by accident never survived that long. They had no means of artificially prolonging life. Every living being had to be able to contribute something to the community, in gratitude for being alive. Even the very old told stories of their heroic past to the young, augmenting the sung history of the professional kriors. Anyone who was completely useless had a way of disappearing. This was very rare though, and it had happened only twice. In both cases, the people concerned had done something so much against the grain of Shavi society that they had simply vanished rather than face ridicule. And as for the very weak, the droughts usually took them away. Thus perfection was bought at a price.

The music changed. The kora singers had stopped, to be followed by the sound of huge drums.

"Now I know we're in Africa," Ronje said.

"Because of the drums?" Mendoza asked.

"Yes. If you want to kill an African culturally, take away his drum."

They all laughed. Flip's eyes strayed to where Anoku the priest was sitting. He sensed that the old man resented their amusement. His skull-shaped head glistened in the silvery light of the moon. Flip watched him closely and, as if in defiance, he went out of his way to whisper something to the man sitting by him. The second man looked in the direction of Andria and

Ista, then a wide cynical smile spread on his face. Flip could guess that, even though the face of Anoku was bland, his thoughts were not very charitable. He didn't have long to ponder on this, because the drums now started to pound in earnest.

King Patayon and his guards entered, and all present bowed to him. Flip bowed without question, hesitating only in case Andria and Ista were being difficult again. He was relieved to see that they had recovered from the earlier scare of the evening. They all bowed and then sat down again, just like everybody else. There was no way they could claim western superiority in Shavi.

King Patayon thanked all the people around him and, gesticulating with the horse tail in his hand towards Flip and the others, said, "I'm giving my wife, Shoshovi, a cow. I've offended her, the mother of my son, the woman who told the world that I'm a man. One should never underestimate the power of women. I only need to offend her once, for her to invoke her sister goddesses to send the albino people. The goddesses have been merciful enough to turn them into friends. I understand that their chief, the one with hair like an utang, is a good cow-herd, too. And that their women enjoy cooking."

The crowd cheered. One of the women was so overcome that she went and embraced Ista and Andria, who now had to join in the fun, even though they could only guess what the jubilation was about.

"I'm going to take Ayi's hardworking daughter as my wife, and because of this Shoshovi will have the fattest cow in Shavi." As the King spoke, they could hear the jingling of bells, and a surly-looking cow, with the same flowers Flip had seen that morning adorning her head, propelled into the gathering.

On seeing the cow, a group of women from where Andria and Ista were sitting came out into the open and started a slow, sensuous dance, teasing with their body cloths, so that one minute the onlooker would think that they were going to expose themselves, the next they would cover themselves as if cold. Now the music was the single voice of the chief kora player, high and poignant. Shoshovi danced round and round the cow that was tightly held by three of the palace boys, as if she were a bullfighter teasing a bull. The song got faster and faster, and suddenly, at a twist in the song, Shoshovi knelt with abruptness in front of the king, and simultaneously the music stopped.

The cheering was deafening. It was a beautiful, graceful dance, of which every movement conveyed a meaning, lost to the outsider. Shavian people expressed themselves in music, dance and song. Shoshovi knew that she was powerless to stop her husband from bringing a ninth woman into the palace and in her dancing she expressed movingly her individuality and that all women, whether the first or the ninth wife, were people, just like men, and her wishes should not be swept aside. She obeyed the precepts of Shavi as the Queen Mother, and Shavi, including her husband, King Patayon, should equally respect her wishes.

"Your wife is delighted with her cow, I see," Egbongbele said in a low voice to his friend, King Patayon.

"She's a good dancer." Patayon's voice cut neatly into his friend's inattention like cold steel on unsuspecting flesh. The cut went deep, making Egbongbele almost jump from his sitting place.

"I still will never learn that the Slow One is one of those people who one minute condemn their women, and the next want them." He shrugged his heavy shoulders. "Settling quarrels between husband and wife has always been a difficult thing. Only a silly person would attempt to do so. I'm talking now like an old fool. Patayon, the Slow One, still cares for and respects his first queen, Shoshovi."

Then aloud, he agreed, "Yes, my friend, our queen is a beautiful and expressive dancer".

10

The Drinks Party

Sunshine streaked the room. Its sharp-fanned fingers slashed across the animal skins on the floor, on which lay Flip, feeling weak, warm and drowsy. As he rolled lazily onto his side, stretching out his arms with the intention of wallowing in the morning's lazy beauty, he felt something stopping his freedom of movement. It felt like a body, and indeed it was, a human body, warm, breathing, alive, and still asleep – Andria's body. Where the hell was he? Oh yes, now he remembered: they were in Shavi. But this was a strange room, definitely not the room that they had had before. This one was lighter, smaller, closer, more intimate and private, just right for a family. And what was Andria doing sleeping next to him with almost nothing on?

Flip's first impulse was to wake Andria, but his methodical mind told him to wait, to give himself time to collect his wits, his manliness and his dignity.

Quietly and gently, Flip got up, and looked around for one of the pieces of cloth he had now learnt to tie about his waist like a towel. Looking around the pale sunlit room, he saw a stool in a corner, an exact replica of the ones they had had in the other room. It was carved out of wood, round in shape with spindly legs. He knew that the seat would have patterns of lizards and birds and leaves of egbo trees. But those were not what interested Flip at the moment. He was much more interested in the neat little pile of body cloth placed on it. He looked around surreptiously to make sure he wasn't being watched, made a dive for a piece of the cloth and tied it around his waist quickly. He could now afford to study the room more closely. Near the stool was a matting partition. He peeped behind it, and there to his delight and relief was Kisskiss, sleeping under a light white cotton cloth, her thumb not far from her mouth. At least she's here, he thought, but then where were the others, Mendoza and his son Dorf, grumpy Ronje and twiggy Ista? Where were they? Why was it that he was here alone with Andria and Kisskiss?

High up on the wall by the curve to his right was an opening, a round window through which the fingers of the early sun entered the room. He stood still and stretched himself to the utmost to make sure he was fully awake and not dreaming. Yes, he was awake alright, the window and the sun's warmth proved it. But he felt a drowsiness of the head and weakness of the knee he associated with love-making. He allowed his mind to dwell on this for a while, while his heart began to beat wildly, as the fantastic idea flashed through his mind again and again, and a peculiar tremulousness took possession of the pit of his stomach. The idea that he had been making love to Andria was reinforced by her nakedness, as she lay face down on the fluffy animal skin. He watched her for a little while with narrowed eyes but could make neither head nor tail of the situation. With a puzzled sigh, he spread a cloth across Andria's back to cover her buttocks. He watched the two mounds of flesh that rose gradually and curved gently into her thighs. He was drowsy, a little weak and somehow this morning felt like a day on which to stay in bed making love. He lay down by her side and supported his head with one hand. But as he lifted his other hand to caress Andria, the picture of Ista, Dorf, Mendoza and Ronje rose in his mind's eye. Moshem, that brilliant and promising young pilot, had died instantly in the crash. He was beginning to accept that death, though Tara's death still hurt badly. But the others were alive and if anything happened to them now, it would be entirely his own fault. He had insisted that the Shavian people were harmless. But who could tell what goes on in the minds of an African tribe?

And yet look at him, the responsible Professor Philip Wagner, being tempted like that Stone Age man from Mesopotania to make love to a woman, simply because the greater part of her body was exposed, whilst he knew nothing of the whereabouts of his other friends. Fear withdrew his tentative hand from Andria's sloping back.

As memory began to return, he felt something must be wrong somewhere. He could now remember last night's party, in honour of the king or chief, Patayon as they called him. He seemed to have married a girl young enough to be his grand-daughter. There had been plenty to eat, and music, drums, koras, and women singing. They had all danced, including Ronje, and had drunk plenty of what tasted like barley beer. They had been given something to chew, which might have been kolanuts. The combination of drink and nuts caused everybody to become happy instantaneously, like stupid drunk children. And then what? There were several live cows, the bride price for the new girl, maybe. Now he understood why they had had to go in the afternoon to fetch the cows, which must be the measure of wealth. And he, Flip, had been honoured, by being taken to a place far beyond the hills and shown where the cows grazed.

He remembered Mendoza's remark, when he'd told him that he'd been to the cow pastures: "To think of you, the great scientist, being reduced to a cow-herd!" Poor Mendoza, he didn't understand the honour that had been bestowed.

Then they had roasted meat of some kind before that horrible sacrifice in which a bird was brutally strangled, and its body flung into the lake. He had felt sick at the time, but the others were all having a good time with the barley beer. He had a feeling that after a while the people were not only laughing with them but at them as well. He had suspected this at the time, but his senses had been too blurred by the barley beer to protest.

Why did they sacrifice a bird when they had so many cows? Had they landed among savages? No, these people were cultured in their own way. One had only to watch and see the way the village was run to know that. He touched his forehead, and realised he was sweating and almost dizzy. He came to the conclusion that the apparently innocent beer and nuts must have contained a powerful drug.

Kisskiss mumbled something in her sleep, turned the other way and pushed the white cloth that covered her body further down, exposing her little chest to the dim morning sunlight. He hoped they hadn't given whatever it was that they'd had to her. He turned around, feeling the light warm air playing about his half naked body and straining his ears for some sound.

"Did everybody have it then?" he asked the silent emptiness. For why else should there have been such an empty stillness?

"Andria! Andria! Wake up. Please wake up," he cried, shaking her gently from side to side. Kisskiss woke first and whimpered from her part of the room.

"Flip, Flip, where . . . what?" the child began drowsily.

"It's alright, Kisskiss, I'm waking your mother. Wake up, Andria, please for God's sake."

Andria eventually yawned and opened her eyes. "Where are we?" she asked sharply, then smiled. "Not in our Newark again?"

"I'm not finding this funny. We're the only people here, the others have disappeared into thin air. I think the whole world has gone to the moon."

"Not the whole world. I can hear Kisskiss and I can hear a hungry goat bleating out there. Aren't they part of the world?"

83

"You know what I mean. Ronje and the others."

"Are you sure Ronje hasn't gone out jogging or chasing that serving girl? He's keen on the native girls."

"That's ridiculous. He hates them."

Andria got up, looked at her scanty clothes and laughed aloud. "Has somebody been undressing me or what? Wait a minute, I was wearing one of those last night . . . " She looked around her in bewilderment. "Flip, Flip, this is a strange house, a new room, I mean."

"Exactly!"

Andria walked over quickly, took a bigger piece of cloth and wrapped it around her, making her look like a fish again. She always did hers wrongly. It didn't suit her like it suited the women of Shavi. She had never mastered the art. For no reason at all, Flip became angry. "Why don't you tie that cloth properly? Even the tiny Shavi girls can do that without any help. I've watched them. It's easy."

"Listen, Philip . . . Wagner. I wasn't born into this."

"You don't have to be born into it. You adapt to it. We've been here for over two weeks, you should be able to do things like that by now."

"We've been here for exactly fifteen days, and I don't see why I should learn to adapt, since I intend leaving this place soon."

Kisskiss came in, holding her own bed cloth over her body. "Andria, Andria. Where's Dorf?"

"Why don't you call your mother, Mum or Ma, like any other child?"

"I don't know what's eating you, Flip. But I like being called Andria."

"Even by your own child?"

The peal of laughter that halted this dialogue was startling, so unexpected that Andria jumped and they all looked towards the door.

Ista was standing there, clutching her cloth around her breast. Everything Ista did, even carelessly, had a touch of sophistication. She held the cloth like a fragile young girl, but ruined the effect by her near hysterical laughter, which emphasised all the bones of her neck, creating a hollow like a tiny water hole. She had tried to twist her hair in a bun at the back of her head, but she'd lost her hair pins in the crash, so her hair, bleached by the sun, escaped from the sole pin and fanned her face. The escaping hair and the hollow in her neck combined to emphasise the delicacy of her face.

"We thought you'd been killed," Ista breathed, widening her liquid-grey eyes.

"Oh, Ista, how could they possibly kill us after all the cows we ate last night? I don't think I can stand meat for another week. By the way, where are Ronje and Mendoza?" Flip asked.

"Mendoza, Dorf and I found ourselves sharing a house. We haven't seen Ronje, and we didn't know where you were, till now. It's all very strange."

"Yes," agreed Andria. "This morning, when Flip woke me up, I didn't know what to think. Ronje's premonition about our being killed kept coming into my mind. It's not a very healthy feeling. But why in the name of God did they separate us? Were we drugged?"

"I think we had too much of the barley beer," Ista said laughing. "It hasn't done us much harm, has it?"

"What of Kisskiss? Did she have it too?" Flip asked, anxiously.

"I think all the children were given a taste as well. It was a celebration after all," Ista said.

"The funny thing was that the Shavians were affected, just like us," Andria said.

"Well," Ista shrugged her thin shoulders. "They're human, so they should be affected, though not to the same degree, because they've been drinking it for ages."

"I still think it's funny," said Andria.

Ista reacted with irritation. "I must say I don't understand you or Ronje. The fact that their culture's different doesn't make us more human than they are."

Andria laughed, and everybody relaxed somewhat. "I don't know about Ronje, but I'll certainly feel happier when I know I can leave this place when I want. I feel so cut off from the rest of the world, not knowing what's happening in Europe."

Flip walked up to Andria and, taking her by the shoulders, shook her in a tender, familiar and possessive way. "Stop worrying, Andria, Europe's still there, I'm sure. And, given time, we'll find a way of leaving here. We're still alive and in the world, aren't we?"

"Sometimes I doubt that very much," Andria persisted.

Flip left her, almost too abruptly, as Ista's watery grey eyes followed his movements, missing nothing. A puzzled frown was beginning to appear on her brow.

Flip changed the subject. "But where's Ronje, if he's not in the same house as you?"

Ista shook her head in mystification.

The low chatter of a group of girls, appearing from another part of the compound, cut short their dialogue. They were bearing some twig sweepers, the kind Ista and Andria had used the day before. They gave one each to Ista and Andria, with a slow smile. They weren't laughing, and one or two of them even looked dour and sleepy.

"What am I supposed to do with this?" Andria cried, holding the twiggy broom away from her body, like a dead rat.

Not understanding what she meant, one of the girls said, "Mesiere," and demonstrated with her own broom what Andria was expected to do with it.

Ista started to laugh again. The girls joined in the laughter, not just because they found the expression on Andria's face funny, but also because they were beginning to like Ista.

"Party's over, dear Andria, now it's work. Women's work, sweeping the compound." The laugh disappeared from her face momentarily as she continued, "This, I suppose, is going to be the pattern".

"You mean they're turning us into white slaves," Andria fumed.

"I don't think so. I think most women do this type of thing here. They haven't got professional street sweepers."

"It's not that bad. In many countries of the world, women sweep the roads," Flip said in a conciliatory tone.

"I want to be able to choose the work I do," Andria retorted.

"Well, that's not possible here. Even if you could make them understand you, they wouldn't need the skills you could offer. So, in this place, you're a road sweeper," Ista said as she shouldered her huge broom and followed the girls out.

"This is reverse discrimination. Here they think we whites are good for only menial jobs . . ." Flip said, laughing.

Ronje and Mendoza suddenly appeared from behind the house occupied by Flip and Andria. Their faces were red with anger. First Mendoza wanted to know what the game was: he had woken that morning next to Ista, he said, casting a wary eye in her direction. Ista blushed violently and looked confused. At this, Flip's mind went back to his awakening to find that Andria was sleeping on the same animal rug as he was. He looked at Andria and saw that she was blushing too. Silence fell as if everybody was thinking the same thing.

Ronje burst out, "They put me in solitary confinement, and this morning those stupid men gave me a hoe. They want to lead Mendoza and me off somewhere. I think they want to make slaves out of us. When a white man lands in a place like this, he is always superior. He makes the native his servant, not the other way round. Flip, you seem to understand them. Why don't you tell them the way things are done in the civilised world? Why don't you explain about being British, and deserving of respect, not like coolies from nowhere?''

''Ronje, I'm sorry, but they wouldn't understand. And even if they did, the skills we can offer in return for their hospitality aren't needed here.''

''Just my luck,'' Mendoza said. ''When I discover a new part of the earth, instead of my lording it over them, they make me a labourer.''

The palace guards arrived and pushed a hoe into Mendoza's and Ronje's hands. They smiled at them lopsidedly, with the same cynical smile Asogba had, and gestured them to follow.

Flip nodded. ''You might as well follow. We don't want trouble. I think I'm being given a day off because of all the work I did on the grazing fields yesterday. I'll spend the time looking around the Newark to see what I can do to make it work.''

''That'll need a micacle. The frame is there, unburnt, the engine could be patched up to fly a short distance – I've already worked on it for a couple of hours. But where do we get oil?''

''If it's reparable, all is not lost. But don't get difficult with those men. I don't think they like you very much,'' Flip warned.

Ronje looked at the guards and muttered, ''The feeling is mutual''.

11
The Rape

Ronje stood on the slopes that led down to the Ogene lakes to catch his breath. Looking to the right, he was faced with undulating hills formed of small rocks and sand, and covered with shrubs, giving the illusion of an unbroken carpet of green. In the centre of the green was the dry patchy area where the people of Shavi lived, among a panorama of pagoda-like buildings with, on the right, the biggest and whitest of the domed houses, the palace. To the left were the smaller ones and, in front of him, he could see the biggest of the Ogene lakes.

Animal sounds were coming from the direction of the lakes. Apart from the discordant sounds of the desert parrots, the atmosphere was peaceful. The sound of frogs and tiny hidden insects harmonised with the landscape.

He stretched out both arms and filled his lungs with air, smiling at the sensation after a punishing run. He'd done it to prepare himself for thinking and worrying about how he was going to get them back to "civilisation". Because he knew that they must get back. They had all been working hard in their spare time on the Newark. And they were lucky that the proud young man, Asogba, had become interested in what they were doing, and had started to help in fetching this and that. It was beginning to look as if he was an important person in the community, able to detail some of his friends to come and work with them. Ronje didn't know the position of the man, but didn't want to find out anyway. He found his loping rickety gait and lopsided smile irritating. In Denmark, where he grew up and in the University of Aarhus where he started his research, he had seldom come across black people. He had started seeing them when he came to England. The woman he married, a South African white, called Shona, loved the black race. In fact, she had left him for a loud mouthed black American from Chicago. This had surprised him at the time – that a beautiful white woman like Shona could go with a black man. He was educated, true, a science journalist, but, blast it, he was uncultivated. He ate too much, he talked too much, he smiled too much, he was larger than life. Ronje hated all these things, and his hatred had been increased by his divorce. At first, he had been happy that Shona wasn't leaving him for another white man – that would have been more humiliating. But later, when he saw her pregnant and looking so happy, relaxed and radiant, he felt betrayed. Nonetheless, he consoled himself that, whatever Shona's new husband was, he was uncivilised and uncultivated, and felt secure enough in his contempt to tell his friends after a few drinks, "Shona prefers to go back to nature". This always elicited sympathetic laughter from his friends.

Ronje sat down wearily by the foot of one of the rocks. His mind reverted unbidden to Shona. Good Lord, that was four years ago. He had since become cynical about women, and when Flip had come up with this idea of escaping the holocaust, he'd thrown himself into it. Flip was another muddle-headed person. A few years before his name had been in all the science journals and he was known as one of the best scientific brains in England. He had given so many pro-nuclear lectures that his name was immediately associated with nuclear missiles. Suddenly he began to change. It was like the conversion of Saul of Tarsus, except that he failed to convince anyone else.

Friends told him that it was too late to tell the ordinary man in the street that all the money spent on nuclear weapons had gone to waste. And how were they going to convince other nations to give up the arms race? Flip was persuaded of the hopelessness of his mission when the Anglican Church Synod gave nuclear build-up its blessing. He had started work on the Newark.

"Did I really believe that we were going to live happily ever after, somewhere out of reach of nuclear fall-out?" Ronje asked himself. He beat his upper arms with his hands to stimulate some warmth. It was not only chilly at this time of the morning in Shavi, it could be cold. But Ronje had discovered that he could bear the rest of the day if he collected this cool feeling inside him. He had enjoyed the regular morning jogs with Flip, until those stupid people decided to marry him to Andria.

At the thought of that episode over two months before, he laughed out loud. Such simple people would never be able to understand that women, grown-up women, could be single. They'd thought Andria was Flip's wife and Kisskiss their child, and that Mendoza was Ista's husband. The funny thing was that with all their scientific know-how, they'd all played along with the game of innocence. Mendoza was becoming really possessive of Ista, who usually hated Mendoza's pomposity and called him a male chauvinist, but now acquiesced in the situation. It was too complicated to explain to the Shavians, so they accepted being happy families. Except for himself, who was now condemned to jogging every morning alone among the rocky hills.

Soon it would be time to pick up his hoe, trek to the water holes and dig the patchy dried-up land. He had managed to plant some flowers at the side of one of the lakes, and had been watering and looking after them, much to the amusement of Asogba. After Shona's desertion, Ronje couldn't stand a black person that behaved the way these Shavi people behaved. They had so much cool and dignity. One only had to watch the meeting of the old men in council to be struck by their self-possession. Sometimes they would sit there for hours, saying very little and staring into vacancy. The young palace guards would stand very still, carrying their hand staffs. That he couldn't bear. He could stand black people behaving badly, because that was expected – volumes had been written about black children's poor performance at school, their disruptive behaviour and so on. But how could one explain the behaviour of blacks that went about their work with dignity? Was it because they had remained in Africa and had never been enslaved in foreign countries? Was that why the people of Shavi were so proud, and none too keen on western civilisation? Ronje's anger coalesced as he thought of Asogba, with his cunning smile, wordless mouth and eyes that could look sharp and gentle at the same time.

He got up and jogged a little further along the snaky path towards the biggest lake. As he arrived at the cool rim of the lake, he stopped abruptly. He was not the only one in search of this seclusion. Somebody was splashing in the water, singing the usual kora monologue the Shavi women sang most of the time. Ronje watched the woman for a few minutes, and for some reason he couldn't understand, a decision arose to possess her. The girl, thinking she was alone, bent and poured water on her honey-coloured body to the melody of her song. She was taking her time, savouring the morning cool. As the water touched her body, she rubbed her sides, as if outlining her curves, and innocently exposed her back. It seemed to Ronje that he had discovered a secret. One minute the women were covered from head to toe in light cotton, then here they were, washing and admiring themselves and singing their sloppy melody. The girl poured a fountain of water over her head, and her voice rose in joy, like an actress at the climax of her act, or

like when Ronje and Shona had climaxed together in the coolness of their sheets.

The girl turned, exposing her front and the blackness of her
nipples, which stood out straight as if pointing at him, the
effect of the cold water she had been pouring on herself.
Ronje's eyes grew wide, and he held the front of his jogging
shorts where he could feel himself shamelessly inflating. He
came out of hiding and said stumblingly, ''Mesiere''.

The girl ran for the piece of cloth she had spread to cool in
the dew and tied it round her waist. Then she saw who it was
and laughed. Ronje laughed too, taking the laughter as an
invitation. He thought 'Black people had no moral standards
anyway. In England and the West Indies, most black women
raised their families alone, because the women slept around,
and the job of looking after themselves and their kids rested on
them'. This one was no different. She'd been enticing him
since he came to Shavi, and was there for anybody to take.
She'd served them when they first arrived, had swept their
compound, and many a time he'd seen her smile in a special
way at the man, Asogba too.''

''An early bath?'' Ronje said in English, gesturing with his
hands so the front of his shorts was exposed.

Ayoko laughed at this, pointing at him and saying, ''To
think my father still maintains that you're not humans! Look
at you, you want a woman. Was that your woman, the one
who died? Poor leper-coloured man.'' She laughed again.

Ayoko should not have laughed, displaying her teeth so
innocently, but she'd never been taught that this kind of teasing could be taken seriously. There had been no need to protect
Ayoko, for since her birth she'd been chosen to be Asogba'a
wife, the next Queen Mother of Shavi. Shavi people gave of
their best to visitors, so she and Shoshovi, the present Queen
Mother, had looked after the albinos when they arrived. They
treated them like anybody else from that day onward. Ayoko

and the Queen Mother had stopped serving them when they became citizens of Shavi, in recognition of their full humanity.

So when Ronje started coming closer to Ayoko, she said, "Don't bother to come down, I've finished my bath, I'm going for my water and then home". Catching sight of Ronje's face, she laughed again, this time instinctively with unease. For the first time, she looked around her to see whether there was anyone to protect her. Then a thought flashed through her mind. Her father had said that these people were another breed of Uthang, and those animals could harm women. Ayoko had never seen a live Uthang before, but this man's eyes were as glazed as those of a dead one brought into the palace by the hunter guards. Her smile faded.

Ayoko was fifteen. She had the slim build of her desert people, with long legs like the giraffes and camels that lived in the savannah around Shavi. She had been cossetted and well-fed, so she was tall for her age, almost as tall as Ronje. But she was thin, unmuscular, and she was innocent.

Ronje fell on her and, in less than ten minutes, took from the future Queen of Shavi what the whole of Shavi stood for. To him, the Shavians were savages and Ayoko was just a serving girl. Though she fought, cried and begged, her pleading was jibberish to him, her resistance enhanced the vengeance he was taking on Shona.

It was soon over, and Ayoko sat on a rock, looking at him. He was no longer human. Her father had been right about the albinos, for what human would rape? She had heard the elders say that things would never be the same after the arrival of the leper people, and now she saw why. What would become of her family? What would they do to her father, who had been going to use her relation to the Royal Family as a means of securing her family for ever? What would happen to her mother and herself? She looked again at the albino. What should she do to him? Kill him? What could she do? She wanted to cry, but her self-possession was too strong. She couldn't go back into her father's house now because she had been defiled. What was she going to do?

She got up, gathered the rest of her clothes and went quietly home.

Ronje ran after her, his hands flailing like the wings of a dying bird, his loose shorts dancing about his wobbly body, the matted hair on his head and chest making him truly resemble an Uthang. "Father was right," Ayoko thought again. "These can't be people – for how could real people go out of their way to destroy the lives of those who have shown them nothing but kindness since they arrived in their midst?"

Ronje was calling after her: "You can come again. We can do it again. I didn't know you were a virgin. But it wasn't so bad, was it? I'll marry you, take you to England, make you a lady. After all, my wife, Shona, married one of your people. I'll marry you . . . I'll learn to love you . . . "

Ayoko did not look back. She walked straight to her mother's house, for this problem was one that was beyond her and she suspected that, despite all her father's authority, this was a problem that would be beyond him as well. In cases of this kind, women should stick together. She went in to her mother, to cry at her breast, the breast that had given her life.

12
Women's War

After Ayoko had told her mother, Siegbo, all, the two women held each other and indulged in bitter tears for a very long time. Then Siegbo wiped her eyes, started to wiggle one of her toes and stared into vacancy. After a while, she sighed. ''What a terrible fate for a little girl like you, my daughter Ayoko. But words are like rags. If you throw them that way, they go there, if you throw them this way, they come here.''

''Should we tell father then?'' Ayoko asked between sobs.

''Your father! Goodness no, Ogene forbid! This is a case beyond men,'' Siegbo smiled. ''You see the men there in council in the palace, their heads bowed, their foreheads creased, and you think they will come up with the 'big solution'. Sometimes they stumble on the right answer, but in most cases they come to the wrong one, like anybody else. We women know when they've made a wrong decision, but as long as no big calamity occurs, we keep quiet to save their face. But this, that has happened this morning, is one thing we can't afford to see muddled. As I said, it's like rags – if we allow men to throw them into the wrong corner, the whole stability of Shavi will be affected. Can you imagine what would happen if it emerged that Ogene hadn't told the truth?''

''How do you mean, mother?'' Ayoko asked, in a small voice.

''Oh, my daughter, many things happened at your birth.

Your father said Ogene had told him that you would be the future Queen of Shavi, and that when you are Queen, Shavi will be blessed. Ever since, we've received cows, grain, everything from the palace because of you. If we disclosed this calamity, Ogene would be proved false, and so would your father, and everybody would start doubting Ogene and wondering why they should obey the King. If we told your father, he would let his anger rule him and do some terrible things to those albinos to get his own back and, after that, what would happen to the rest of us? No, my daughter, we've never had a case like this in Shavi before, so we women will deal with it. It is our war.''

Ayoko watched as her mother went into her room, took out her outdoor cloth and wrapped it around her plump body with jerky determined movements, muttering to herself all the while. Ayoko could hear her saying, "Ogene, you are a woman, you should understand". When she came out, she said, "Ayoko, wipe your tears and go about your work as if nothing had happened".

Ayoko's eyes opened wide. "What, mother, are you asking me to go on and prepare food for father? Ogene would kill me. I have been polluted. I mustn't go near the palace."

Siegbo looked at her fifteen-year-old daughter, beautiful, young, trusting and pure, and felt proud of her. She had raised her in the culture of the land, taught her what was right and wrong without any shades of grey. For the first time, she was confronted with human dirt, evil, indignity and violation. For this, she would need a new set of rules, which Siegbo had not taught her. Time was too short to start that now. They must act quickly to save the fabric of Shavi life. So she said, "My daughter, I think your father was right. Those leper-looking creatures are not human. You can only be violated by humans. Animals cannot violate human beings, because there are no such laws in the animal kingdom. So say nothing to anybody.

97

Go in and wash yourself properly and go about your work. Leave the rest to me. You have not been violated. The creature, Ronje, is an animal, for what human would destroy a beautiful person like you? And we can't let an animal destroy you, daughter of the great priest of Ogene, the would-be Queen Mother. Do you not know that after the next dry season, you are moving into the palace so that my grand-children will one day reign in Shavi? Dry your tears, daughter, and go about your work with a young bright face. Leave the war to us, the mothers.''

Tears sprang from Ayoko's eyes and fell on her breasts. She saw her mother transformed into a warrior. She took the two short steps that separated them, hugged her tightly and said, "Yes, mother. I'll do what you say. Only an animal could behave the way that man behaved towards me''.

Siegbo smiled and thought to herself, ''Poor child, she's learning very, very fast. Rape ages and humiliates any woman, young or old''.

Shoshovi, surprised to see Siegbo come to visit her so early in the morning, asked if all was well with her household. The two senior women of Shavi were so bowed down with domestic responsibility, that they seldom had time to sit and talk. This, then, was a great opportunity, and Shoshovi in her exuberance would not hear of Siegbo going without being properly entertained. Siegbo allowed herself to be indulged. She accepted honeyed goat meat with spices, strong drink made from coffee beans, and jenja nuts.

But as soon as she started her story, Shoshovi sat up with jerky suddeness, and became abruptly militant. Siegbo watched the laughter lines around the corners of her mouth sag, before they firmed to lines of determination. She nodded her head vigorously at all Siegbo's plans.

Presently she spoke in a forced whisper. ''We don't kill humans in Shavi, but we do sometimes kill animals for sacrifice to Ogene, or for food. And you know my friend that animals, once they have tasted something they think is good, will always come back for more, and if they fail to get it, they wander around snatching their pleasure anywhere. It's Ayoko today, tomorrow maybe it'll be my daughter, the princess Ama. I'm glad you haven't told any of the men. You're right, we must purify our land. This is our war.''

Ronje was busy the rest of the day, tidying the water hole and working in the fields. He never liked the job, but there was an intrinsic satisfaction in handling and touching natural things. He still had his paunch, which didn't look as if it would diminish, due to his taste for the jenja drink which Ista had rightly called barley beer. He was having his usual rest after the day's work when Flip came to him.

"Sorry to have to wake you, Ronje," Flip began, clapping his hands at the door in the Shavian manner.

"Oh, don't mind me, old boy. Should have been up long ago. This place makes one deliciously tired, have you noticed? So tired that one doesn't feel guilty, sleeping around the place''

Flip laughed. "Sleeping around the place. You've not been doing that here, have you, Ronje?"

"Of course not," Ronje snapped.

"Well, I think you're tired because on top of your work, you still do your morning jog everyday, don't you?"

Ronje sat upright. Had the girl Ayoko reported him? Did Flip know? He got up from his sitting position and walked mechanically to a corner, stopped and deliberated with his back to Flip. He pretended to be going through the act of putting on a shirt, one of the few he had saved from the Newark. The others had lost most of their clothes, with the exception of the light pressure suits they wore, which were quite unsuitable for this climate.

"I don't know how you can cope with shirts in this place. I find them too close, one needs freedom here."

"Why won't he get on with what he wants to say? He's going to accuse me of raping a silly serving girl. These people are so simple, I can't imagine they'd mind that much. The girl is probably a servant of some kind." If Flip was here to admonish him, he was going to remind him that it was alright for him, since the Shavians had married him to Andria. Nobody thought of him. How come these people hadn't matched one of their women with him? Even Mendoza had Ista. He was quite sure that those two made love to each other because Ista had stopped calling Mendoza a brute. So none of them had any right to admonish him for sleeping with a serving girl. But Flip was biding his time, talking about shirts. So he replied in kind, "Well, I still have a few good ones".

"Save those shirts for when we decide to go. Even women can wear shirts on top of the sheet of cloth. It'll be a new fashion in Europe." He laughed at his own joke.

Ronje turned round hurriedly. "When?" he cried, "When are we leaving?"

Flip's usually calm face wrinkled itself in amusement. Then, as if at a loss what to do with his hands, he started to stroke his beard. "In time, in time, and sooner than you expected."

"Mind you, this isn't a bad place," Ronje began, in an attempt to regain his composure, for he had seen Flip's amused smile. "After a while, one might even get used to the simplicity of life here. One thing I notice is that it's difficult for humans to sink below the level they're used to. It's easier to aspire higher, if you understand what I mean. I like the therapeutic feeling I get from working with my hands for a while, but when it goes on and on, it becomes a bore."

"Ah, this place may be geographically a desert, but not culturally. It's very rich in their own semi-nomadic culture. In fact, I intend coming back and studying the life of the people. Now King Patayon has paid for his new bride, his son, Asogba, with the lopsided smile, is going to start buying and selling cows to pay for his bride and future Queen Mother, Ayoko. The marriage has been planned a long time . . . Ronje, what's the matter with you?''

Ronje's legs were giving way. He rested his elbow on the round ledge that led to the only open space in the round wall of his room. ''I'm fine, Flip. Still dizzy from sleep, that's all.''

Flip's earlier amused wrinkles now gave way to deep corrugated furrows. ''If you feel this weak, maybe Ista should come to have a look at you. You look . . . well, somehow not your usual self.''

Ronje managed a smile. ''You think I'm not myself because I said I might come to like this place? Well, we've been here almost three months now, and nothing horrible has happened so far.''

''I suppose you're right,'' Flip said, in a retiring voice. ''I came to tell you that we'll be going to the cow market tomorrow. You know that I'm one of the Ministers for Cows, a kind of treasury employee. I haven't got the faintest idea where the market is, but it'll take us three days to get there, and three days to get back. I'd like you and Mendoza to continue refining that oil. I've inspected last week's effort and the results are very promising.''

''You mean, Flip, that we'll be able to fly an areoplane on date oil? What a breakthrough in the history of aviation!''

''Where there's a will, there's a way, my dear Ronje. And it's either that or live here forever. I know how exhausting it is in the evenings, but a couple of hours every day will do the trick.''

''Hmmm.''

''I wouldn't mind living here forever. I'm so tired of our nerve-racking life. But I feel I should help you all back to Europe since I spearheaded the idea of coming out in the first place. I will forever blame myself for that.''

''Oh, come off it, Flip. We're all grown people. We chose to go along with the idea, remember. I know that at times we haven't made life easy for you, but if you think for a moment that you forced me into this, you're wrong, old chap. I went into it with my eyes wide open. I'm glad in a way that the old world is still standing. It must be, or we'd have felt the effects here, however remote and sheltered this place is."

"Sometimes I think we should blow ourselves up, and give Mother Africa an opportunity to produce a new set of humans, better equipped to cope with the world. All we've so far produced are instruments of physical and moral destruction,' ruminated Flip.

"Moral destruction?"

"Well, yes, Ronje, look at this place. When we came here, they made the best of their women, the would-be Queen Mother, look after us before they could even be sure we were humans like them. They had no way of knowing, because we don't speak the same language, but they trusted us with their best. Can you imagine the Princess of Wales leaving her palace home to go and look after uninvited non-English speaking visitors?"

Ronje laughed, despite himself. "In the first place, they'd be guests of Her Majesty at Clerkenwell Prison and then deported home. Yes, you're right there. But why are these people different?"

"Because to them we're all immigrants. They came here first, that's all. We're free to stay and work and contribute to the richness of their culture."

"But it's like that in England and America too, almost everybody is an immigrant . . . "

"And when you look at it on the global level, we're none of us here for more than the proverbial three score years and ten."

"Flip, how have you managed to learn so much about the people of Shavi? I've only mastered a few words."

"I wanted to learn about them, so they taught me, especially my friend, the Prince Regent, Asogba. We talk for long periods of time, looking after the animals. He's a great philosopher.''

There was a pause. Then Flip said, "I must go now. My wife will be wondering where I am."

"It's nice, isn't it, Flip, for you and Andria, living like husband and wife?"

"I know, we're loving it. My fear is that it's too easy to get the women pregnant in a place like this. They lost their pills in the crash. But I wouldn't mind, not really."

"Oh, Flip, but you swore you wouldn't bring a child into this violent world."

"Ah, not this world, not this Shavian world. I meant our own polluted world, where the acquisition of money reigns supreme."

Flip walked towards the door, holding his body cloth gracefully as if he'd been born with it. Ronje marvelled at the man's adaptability. He wondered whether it would be right to let him know what he had done to Ayoko this morning. He never knew that a group of people could be so trusting as to expose the future hope of their land to strangers. They even exposed their wealth to Flip, who had not, however, abused their trust. Ronje had.

"Flip, could one of us marry one of the native women?"

"Do you want to marry one of them? I thought you didn't like this place."

"I mean if one had to marry."

"What do you mean, had to?" Flip asked.

"Well . . . you know, in case we can't leave soon, or something like that."

"And when we do leave, would you take her with you? Mind you, it's happening in many countries, blacks marrying whites and vice versa. Look at your former wife, Shona."

"I know all about her!"

"I'm sorry, I don't mean to bring that up. What I'm saying is, that if you contemplate anything like that here, it must be for real. They don't divorce. And you have to work for cows to pay the bride price. That's their way of testing a man's integrity. If you can work for cattle, you can look after a family. Have you any girl in mind? Most are probably betrothed."

"Not really, but I was thinking of that serving girl . . . "

"She's not a serving girl!" Flip's voice rose. "And, Ronje, before you endanger the lives of the rest of us, never, never think about that girl. She's the daughter of the only powerful man in Shavi who still views us with suspicion, and is being trained by the Queen Mother, Shoshovi, to be the wife of the prince. Just forget her, she's not for you to take. She's been specially trained to be friendly, but that doesn't mean she's looking for a husband. Please, Ronje, leave her alone. I don't want us to introduce our corrupt ways to this people."

"Alright, alright, I only asked, since you know so much about them."

"Ayoko is the symbolic Mother of Shavi. If you rape her, you rape Shavi."

"Who's talking of rape?" Ronje asked, in a quivering voice, turning his back on Flip. "I asked about marriage. After all, you all have a wife now."

"Help Mendoza with the date oil refining, Ronje. I must get you away from this place."

"The Newark isn't going to take us very far. Have you thought of that, Flip?"

"It can fly at least two hours, and I'm sure we're not too far into the Sahara."

And Flip left Ronje.

"Now, what am I supposed to feel about all this? Flip's right. We must leave here. And I must find a way of talking to that girl, to stop her exposing me."

13
Ronje Disappears

The ground was wet with dew when Ronje set out on his morning jog. He had hardly slept the night before, tossing this way and that, thinking of the best way to handle the situation. Flip had made the people of Shavi out to be a chosen race. Ronje had believed him at first, but had to laugh after a while at his own stupidity. Flip was a romantic. How could the people of Shavi be that important if no one had ever heard of them? They didn't even know of the existence of other races, except those distant tribes that bought their cattle. Why should he be unduly worried about sleeping with one of their girls, and one who had been making eyes at him since their arrival?

Nonetheless, Ayoko dominated his thoughts that night. He had talked to Flip of marrying her. Now he thought he must have been raving mad. How could he have married a girl who only knew how to fetch water, sweep compounds and had few words, apart from her smiles and her "Mesieres"? He would have left her behind, of course, when they managed to repair the Newark. There had been cases like that in many parts of the world, like West Africa, Vietnam and even the Pacific Islands, where there are many pale skinned people whose fathers were Europeans. Why then should this place be different? Flip and his illusion of the noble savage!

Flip had started their relationship with the people of Shavi on the wrong footing. They were Europeans, after all, and it

105

had always been the duty of Europeans to impose their culture on whoever they came in contact with. Flip had allowed the white race to be degraded. Fancy turning him into a waterhole attendant and a farmer! It was alright for Flip, who had wanted Andria for a very long time. Now they had virtually married her to him, and turned him into a cowboy, Flip was enjoying himself. The only compensation Ronje could see for himself was this girl, Ayoko, and Flip wanted to deprive him. He wasn't going to let him. He was going to the spot where he had had her yesterday, and wait for Ayoko to come. Since she hadn't told her people, and had smiled at him whenever they met, she couldn't have hated him that much.

He would talk to her in the limited words they had. He would civilise her, and, if he could convince her parents, she could come and live with him. Ronje didn't think that someone like Ayoko could have the dignity not to want him. She was a black girl from the desert, an object of use for any white male wanderer. He had only done what generations of his race had done before.

Ronje didn't reckon with the force of the women of Shavi, Shoshovi, Siegbo, Iyalode and the older palace queens, who had all gone to the Ogene lakes to make a pact to silence. A dog that bit a human must be put down. There was only one concession – if Ronje did not appear on the same spot within the next seven days, they would know that he had repented. Then they would meet again and think of their next strategy. Meanwhile, Shoshovi urged everybody to bring their fishing nets.

So, early the following morning, the older women of Shavi, with Iyalode the bald priestess of Ogene, went out in the dark, cold morning, to the same spot by the smaller lakes and hid by the rocky dunes and waited. There was little to give the women protection but the rocks. They crouched, their old limbs aching. Most were in their late forties, one or two in their fifties, old for Shavi. But they were determined women who had given birth to sons and daughters, and had become the pillars of Shavi. So they waited.

Ronje felt neither the touch of dew in the air, nor the mist, nor the cold. He trotted round the smaller lake several times to gain thinking time. A heap of stones that over the years had weathered the wind and formed themselves into conic-shaped dunes clustered the entrance of what Ronje had now come to call the grove. This was the secluded spot Ayoko had chosen for her bath yesterday. The buzz and whisphers of the morning animals and insects were subdued by the misty air. It was unearthly quiet.

As he trotted along, his sandalled feet falling and rising along the sandy grove, one could understand why Ayoko had found him disturbing and had innocently smiled at him. Even the crouching women sighed, knowing that they were going to destroy such a specimen of health, strength and manliness. His shorts, now clammy from sweat, clung to his anatomy, and his hair was matted. He jogged, oblivious of the calamity he had caused and the calamity he was soon to face. When he thought he heard something move, he stopped running and started to call gently, "Ayoko, Ayoko, come out of hiding". He listened and was sure he could sense somebody there. He called again and again, and, getting no answer, shrugged his shoulders. "If you want to play hide and seek, I don't. I want to explain things to you, that's all."

Ronje turned to go. Then he felt himself falling, hitting his head on one of the protruding rocks. For a few seconds, he lost consciousness. Then pains like needles started to shoot through the whole of his body and he saw himself in a net, and hooded figures dragging him behind them. He began to shout, "Stop, stop it. Where are you dragging me to? Stop, stop!"

As soon as he started to cry out, the women started to run, dragging Ronje with them. Ronje made desperate attempts to free himself from the net, but he would need a tool to cut the wiry strings. Soon he stopped crying out. He was beginning to lose his voice, and his energy, and was bleeding profusely.

The women walked on for about an hour to an open space where there was not a single tree, but miles and miles of rocky sand. Here they stopped. They made sure that the net was tight, so that there was no way for Ronje to escape, without outside help. They didn't beat him, or club him, or say a word to him. They simply left him there for the desert vultures, turned back mutely and went to their homes.

When they got home, their families noticed how exhausted they looked. When asked, they simply replied: "We went to make sacrifices to Ogene."

Mendoza and the palace guards wondered what had happened to Ronje for a while but they concluded that, since he didn't like the farming work all that much, he must have gone with Flip. With that conclusion, they temporarily forgot Ronje and concentrated on the work of repairing the Newark.

14
Flip Returns

By the evening of the third day, Flip hadn't returned as expected. The remaining members of the Newark flying club in Shavi were eaten up with worry, rendering them limp and lethargic. They didn't know where to start looking for Flip and Ronje. Ronje could have told them that he was going to the cattle market with Flip, but that was Ronje all over – temperamental and unpredictable.

For no reason at all, they suddenly found the repair work on the Newark exhausting. They agreed to give it a miss for a while. Andria and Kisskiss also asked if they could move in with Mendoza and Ista. "If they aren't back after two days, we'll have to assume they've come to some harm," said Mendoza.

"But these people are friendly. You couldn't meet friendlier people. All this can't be just a show for our benefit. They're sincere, I feel it," Ista declared vehemently.

"Then why aren't the others here?" Mendoza asked.

"There must be an explanation. They said they'd be back early this morning. It's only late evening, they're probably delayed. Let's just wait and see."

Andria couldn't help but admire Ista's faith. She looked around her house and admired Ista's attempts to make it like a home. Furnishing the one large room demanded every creative fibre. She had sewn different goatskins to look like rugs, and had put strings through some of the pieces of body cloth, to make curtains for the holes that served as windows. Andria smiled as her eyes went around the apartment.

"And that's not all," Ista enthused. "I'm collecting birds feathers to make soft pillows, instead of those rocky head rests." Nobody said a word for a while, and Ista felt she had to add apologetically. "Might as well make us comfortable while we're here".

"I can't understand how you can be thinking of such things in a place like this, Ista. All my thoughts are about going home!" said Andria.

"I think it's due to my upbringing. My father was a doctor too, remember? But he didn't practice in Germany. He went to the Sudan, then to Nepal."

"He probably didn't like the orderly life," Mendoza said, with a forced smile.

"You may be right, John, because he kept saying that he would go back to his birthplace, but he never did. He didn't last long enough."

Andria was still worrying about Flip. "Suppose Flip doesn't come back, where will we start looking for him?" she asked.

"He'll come back," said Ista reassuringly. "He went to the cattle market, and I'm sure Ronje is there with him too, delaying their progress. He didn't like his work here and he didn't like walking either. Flip's different. They seem to regard him as being more charismatic than any of us, and take him for our leader. They call him chief – "eze" – the same word they use to refer to King Patayon. So they won't harm him. They're in fact showing Flip their secrets."

"An incurable optimist in whom there is no suspicion," teased Andria. "Suppose we proved later to be their enemies and here to spy on their activities?"

"They probably don't see any reason why anyone should

want to harm them," Ista said, passing round some of the goat's meat she had roasted.

"A bit naive though."

"And risky."

"I know, but you can tell that somewhere in their past, they've been nomadic people, who trusted in the goodness of others for survival. They probably discovered this hidden place by sheer accident. It's secluded, and the surrounding hills have protected it from the direct effect of the desert air. And they have a fairly constant supply of water."

"I understand that during some bad droughts the water level can be uncomfortably low and so bad that they have to water their cattle and their surviving vegetation from the same source," said Mendoza.

Andria nodded. "The water from the small lakes is for washing and bathing, the water from the big one for drinking. But some of those small ones are very low already. And apart from the few heavy rains we had when we came here almost three months ago, there've been scarcely any rains at all," she said.

"The more I study them, the more I suspect that constant fear of the drought has given them this sensitive profound air, which is so disarming," Ista said appreciatively.

This made Mendoza start one of his joyless dry laughs. "You're both learning fast, if you don't mind my saying so."

"We find your patronising air very touching," retorted Ista.

"Well, he's succeeded in turning you into a wife and mother, and if John Mendoza can achieve such a feat with you, I suppose he thinks he has the right to be patronising to all women. After all, Ista, you're regarded as one of the hardest nuts of the species!"

"We're in Rome, so we do what the Romans do," smiled Ista. "I sometimes wonder why they didn't pair me up with Ronje."

"I think Ronje resents that. He's been going about like an angry bull ever since," said Andria.

"Yes, but I really don't know why they paired me off with John," said Ista.

"I think I know. Dorf looks like his father and you remember that on our first few days when Kisskiss was ill, you kept holding Dorf, so they must have thought you were his mother, and Mendoza his father. The same yardstick was applied to Flip and me and Kisskiss. I don't think Flip minded very much, it's just that I'm still doubtful about the restraining bonds of marriage."

"Well, you've had a trial one now. Will you marry him when you both get back to Ontario? Has he ever asked you, Andria?"

Andria laughed. "He hasn't proposed yet, but he keeps hinting."

They talked and ate far into the night, until the owls started to make their mournful sounds, and the darkness descended. In Shavi it was never completely dark, because even on moonless nights, the grey rocks were always faintly luminous. But when there was a moon, everything, the home houses, the trees, and even human shadows, had a silvery tinge. This night though was moonless.

Soon the conversation flagged, the air again became heavy with worries and fear. Three months ago, they had lost Moshem and Tara. Now were they losing Ronje and Flip? Flip was romantic to a fault. No doubt he was intrigued by the freshness of the people of Shavi, but he was too trusting. How on earth could he tell what they were thinking or what they would do to him? He didn't seem to care for his own safety, and would be even more surprised to know that Andria worried about him. He felt he was free, but at times a feeling of being answerable for his colleagues and humanity at large would come over him, hence the building of the Newark to save his friends. His policy with the Shavians was simple and uncomplicated: since they had no means of leaving immediately, and no weapons with which to fight, their best survival strategy was to play along with them, until they could make the Newark fly again. He had explained this to Mendoza often, but what disturbed the others was that he was playing the role as if he liked it.

Andria was sure Flip was enjoying himself. She had never seen him so relaxed. She had woken in the night many a time to see him flat on his back sleeping like a child with his bearded mouth half open, and if she made a move that woke him, it was time to make love. She didn't mind that either; in fact, she noticed that the more their familiarity grew, the better he became. But she feared pregnancy and had told him so. All he had said was, "You think I'm too irresponsible to look after my own child?" and the conversation had been dropped. She wouldn't be surprised if she were pregnant now – the more reason why she'd like to leave.

"Mendoza, I think we have to find out what has happened to my Shavian husband. I have the right to know. This place makes one pregnant, just like that, and it's going to be almost too late to do anything about it when we get back to civilisation, if we ever do."

Ista's eyes were wide open. "I'm beginning to feel pregnant too. I didn't want to alarm anybody unduly, so I've kept it to myself."

"What are you two talking about, being pregnant like the native women? I thought you as a doctor should know better."

"I know, but you see, my dear Mendoza, I'm a woman too, and human, and can't stop my body from doing the work it was originally created to perform. In short, our pills got destroyed with the fire in the Newark."

The three of them walked gingerly over the rocks, in and out of the shadows, until they came to the house near the palace, the house of Egbongbele. Through gesticulation, they finally made Egbongbele's wives understand what they were asking for. With a lot more gesticulation, Egbongbele's household told them that Asogba and his group were not back yet. One of the women tried to inform Andria that her own son was with the group as well.

"Is our friend Ronje with them too?" Mendoza repeated, drawing Ronje's figure in the air. He was greeted with laughter by the women who didn't know what he was getting at. They thought him very funny indeed.

Andria and her friends had to be satisfied with that. "I'm sure Ronje must have gone with them. Where else could he have been? But he should have told us," Andria said, in a low voice.

"Those slave drivers wouldn't have let him if he'd breathed a word of his intention. They need us to tend their water holes. Now I wish I'd gone with them too, at least it would have given me an idea as to our location," said Mendoza.

"And then we'd have been left here at their mercy," Andria said with resignation.

"You still don't trust them, do you, Andria?" Ista asked.

"Oh, Ista, I'm so mixed up, I don't know what to believe. I want Ronje and Flip back, and us all to be home, or somewhere people understand our language."

When the clapping of hands which Flip had now adopted as a way of announcing his presence was heard early the next morning, it was Kisskiss who ran to the door. When she saw Flip, she shouted joyfully, "They're back, Flip and Ronje are back! Andria, Aunt Ista, wake up!"

Flip's smile was broad as he picked up Kisskiss and gave her the usual swing. "You'll soon be too big for swings, Kisskiss, especially as I'm getting so old now."

"You're not really old. Please give me another, and another..."

The others woke. They looked quite a picture as they stood there clutching their night cloths about them. Flip looked at their relieved faces and cried, "You haven't been worrying about us, have you? Oh yes, we were delayed. We had to walk most of the way, you know, and walking long distances can be exhausting, for an old man like me. They're all used to it. Heh, don't I deserve a kiss for being back and bringing Ista this?"

Andria hastily tied her night cloth around her neck and flung her now free arm around Flip's neck, crying, "Flip, I'm glad you're back. We all are. We couldn't sleep last night, oh Flip, it was so terrible. Please next time try to phone ... no, not phone. Oh, let's go back to our house before I talk myself silly."

"Heh, that's alright. We're back, so why the tears?" Flip asked, looking nonplussed. He freed himself from Andria, walked stiffly up to Ista and placed a colourful necklace of beads around her neck. He stepped back to see the effect and cried, "I knew you'd love it. I think they're unique".

Ista felt her neck and agreed. "I've never seen a necklace made of leather beads before. I'll always treasure this, Flip, thanks a lot".

"You're very welcome. Come on, wife, come on, Kisskiss, home, let's go home."

The three of them wrapped their cloths tighter around their bodies, put on the specially made leather slippers they wore in Shavi and were about to leave the house when Ista remarked, "Ronje is always a strange man. Shouldn't he have taken the trouble to tell us that he would be going to the cattle market with you? We were out of our minds with worry."

Flip came back into the room and stared at them.

"He went with you, didn't he?" Andria's voice was tight, hoarse and low.

"I saw Ronje last four days ago when I went to tell him that

I would be going to the cattle market with Asogba and the others. I told him to help you with the refining of the date oil. I haven't seen him since. He didn't go with us.''

"Now that's very strange, because even the Shavians didn't know where he was last night. We took it for granted that he went with you," said Mendoza.

Flip, as he was wont when baffled, held his beard, which was now caked with dust. "Ronje's always strange, but I must admit he was stranger when I last spoke to him," he said.

"Really? What did he say?" Ista asked, in bewilderment.

"He asked about the possibility of marrying Ayoko," Flip replied, still holding tight to his beard, as if for support.

"And did you tell him he could?" Mendoza persisted.

"I told him that Ayoko is the future Queen Mother, the betrothed of Asogba, and I told him that contemplating anything with the girl would be asking for trouble. So I advised him to help you on the Newark, before he landed us all in trouble. That I found very, very strange."

"That Ronje should think of that at all is rather odd, since he hates the people and the place," Mendoza said.

"I hope they haven't executed him for committing what they regard as an abomination," fretted Andria.

"I don't think so. He was asking me about it. He didn't say he had actually done anything, and I saw Ayoko this morning. She was one of the women who came to meet us. I don't think he would be so stupid."

Ista sighed. "Ronje's a muddled-up person. I wonder if he would tell anyone if he'd done a thing like that. I just wonder."

"Stop wondering, Ista. I'm sure he's alive and well in his house. But we'd better warn him again, and hurry the work on the Newark. These people may be easy-going, but I fear that if anyone tampers with the daughter of their chief priest, they're asking for trouble. And we can't afford any trouble," Mendoza concluded.

15
Ayoko's Secret

It was late evening and Anoku the chief priest had had a really tiring day. He'd been up early, to make sacrifices to the big lake, which the King had asked him to do in order to find out about the disappearance of one of the albino people, the one they called Ronje. It had puzzled them all. One minute he was there, the next he had vanished. He had tried to convince himself that no-one in Shavi had anything to do with the man's disappearance, but somehow he couldn't be sure that this was the case. Everybody in Shavi knew Anoku hadn't liked the arrival of the albinos, but he wouldn't go as far as to harm a single hair on any of their heads, since they had been unanimously accepted as humans. The King didn't say he suspected Anoku, he had simply said through Egbongbele, "Anoku, one of the men has disappeared mysteriously. Maybe you can find out what's happened to him."

Anoku had felt like shouting to establish his innocence, but this wasn't the way things were done in Shavi. So he waited, counting his fingers and muttering to himself. Then he asked, "Where does the council want me to start my search?"

Mensa, the great council talker, had at this point asked permission to speak. He reminded Anoku of his powers and his duty, and the fact that he was Ogene's spokesman on earth. He said that Anoku's question was irrelevant. The King was to rule, and Anoku was to search and pray about anything mysterious.

Anoku had looked up, the veins on the side of his head showing in criss-cross patterns as he chewed and spat. A thin man, he was always chewing jenja, and, with his hair completely shaved, reminded one of a walking dead. He peered ghoulishly at the king and his men and said, "I will ask the Ogene goddess". His dry answer had settled the matter at the time.

He had now spent over ten days, killing fowls and birds, praying and concentrating hard on what could have happened to the albino, but still he was none the wiser. Tomorrow, the Shavi rest day, Ibu day, he would be expected to make a speech about all he had found. Each family had contributed a bird at least, and therefore he wasn't going back to tell them that he didn't know what had befallen the albino.

He was now on his way home, taking a short cut to his dwelling. He didn't want to go the palace way, even though that route was flatter and less laborious, so he took the hilly, rocky way. Stopping for breath on this near dark evening, he was surprised to see bright lights coming and going from the place of the albino's crash. Being tired as well as curious, he sat down wearily on a clump of stones and watched. While he was deep in concentration, noting every move of the albinos and Asogba's helpers, the talk he was going to give the council came to him.

The albinos weren't stupid. He had sensed their intelligence right from the day they landed. If he was going to have a rival in holding the thoughts of the people of Shavi, it was going to be from them. Yet how could he control people whose past he didn't know? If he wanted to prevent anyone in Shavi from venturing out into a strange domain, he only had to consult Ogene and tell them that some evil would befall them. In nearly all cases, he was listened to, and the adventurous youth's curiosity was curbed. For any youth that showed an over-restless spirit, he recommended marriage, which meant his working hard for months or even years to raise enough cows for the bride's dowry. In this subtle way, he controlled Shavi. The King knew it, and so did his assistant and priestess, Iyalode, and they kept silent. The priestess was better at this than he was. He had nearly lost control, many a time, like the day the albinos arrived.

He watched them now, busily coming and going, and something told him that if they could devote so much time to the water-coloured bird, it could only be because they were sure it would work. He had been to the bird himself, had fingered its exterior. It was like iron. Some parts of it had been damaged by the fire when it nosedived at Shavi, but it had kept its shape. Now they were trying to rebuild it, so tomorrow he would first tell the council that the missing albino's whereabouts would be revealed in time, then he would go on to tell them what he thought was the most urgent preoccupation – whether or not the albinos' bird would fly again. He would urge that if it happened, the Shavians should not prevent them from going. He knew he couldn't prevent them from going, unless he ordered the bird to be burned, and even his son, Kwesi, would go against him if he did that. So he would tell the council that Ogene gave her blessing to their work, that one day they would go, and maybe come again to visit them with bounty and gifts. That way, he could tie the whole troublesome episode up nicely.

Anoku got up, still slightly tired, but refreshed. He still had over two hundred fowls and birds in his house. He would tell his wife, Siegbo, to roast a hundred, to spice them with jenja nuts and send them to the palace for the council members to refresh themselves with whilst he delivered his speech, which he knew would take a whole day. At this hopeful thought, his face brightened in the dark evening, and his walk down the hill was livelier than before.

"It's a lovely night, our priest," Asogba's voice cut through his happiness. Anoku stopped. One didn't immediately answer people, even if one knew the person addressing one was the prince. "Is it the son of Patayon?" he queried.

"Our priest, I wish you good evening," responded Asogba.

"Hmmm," Anoku drawled, contemplating the starry sky. "You're right," he answered eventually. "This night is beautiful. Are you coming from the albino people?"

"Yes. I've been helping them. I want to learn their wizardry."

"Hmmm, it won't do you any harm, Asogba. Have a good night."

"Good night to you, our priest."

Anoku knew that he'd been right. He also knew that Asogba had a way of getting what he wanted. He hurried home to get everybody in his house ready. One thing he was going to make perfectly clear was his innocence concerning the missing albino. He and his family had nothing whatever to do with it.

Anoku hurried his household through the night's preparations. He was going to foretell the future in grand style, after which his family would be richer by about a hundred birds and fowls, which the priest's family was permitted to eat. He knew that the albino people would soon want to go, especially after the mysterious disappearance of their friend.

Shoshovi hadn't known that her husband would take the disappearance of the man so seriously. Men were strange, one minute they were all sure that the albinos had no souls, the next they were all worrying about the disappearance of a souless creature.

All the women involved had their hearts in their mouths when Patayon ordered the palace guards to scour the environs of Shavi. They searched everywhere, but there was no sign of Ronje. This surprised Siegbo when she met Shoshovi on the seventh day.

"Do you think Ogene has intervened and spirited the albino devil away?"

Shoshovi screwed up her face, placed her finger on her mouth as if about to whistle for the palace dog and nodded. "You see, my friend of many years, the voice of the women is the voice of Ogene. I don't know what would have happened to us otherwise, especially now that the albino chief is becoming more and more popular with our farmers and ordinary people.

"I noticed that too, and I hope Anoku doesn't start being jealous."

"Don't be frightened about that, my friend. Your husband isn't a fool. He knows when to blow with the wind. Isn't he still praying to Ogene to show him a sign as to where the albino is?"

Both women burst into laughter.

"Here, my friend, eat jenja nuts. Let your husband go on praying and killing fowls. That at least will occupy everybody's mind. By the time ten days have passed, that wicked creature will have gone back to his ancestors, if he ever had any."

Though Siegbo was thus pacified, she still worried, particularly about her daughter. It was true that the albinos hadn't brought anything that spread quickly and openly like leprosy. But they had brought other things – new ideas and strange ways. The more one tries to caution youth against a new phenomenon, the more they want to know about it.

Ayoko who had cried all night after her rape, thought deeper than any girl of her age. How was her mother going to cover up this calamity? If all went well and she didn't get pregnant, what would happen on the day of their age group's clitorisation? How would she explain the fact that she wasn't a virgin? The Queen Mother and all the other women who performed the ceremony would know. And another thing, hadn't they told her that if a girl was not clitorised, a man couldn't enter her? But the stupid albino did. He entered, he kept her there, until she had no strength left. That again was not true.

Her mother had disappeared early the following morning, and hadn't returned until midday. She'd told her that the albino had been taken care of, the way any animal would be. Ayoko knew exactly what she meant. They set large wire nets to catch animals, but not for people. Ayoko knew the albino was a person. Her mother and the other women had used the tag of "creature" to pacify their conscience. Now she started to worry and cry afresh. Suppose the women had killed a man for her sake? Whatever had happened, it was a secret that would remain with her all her life. She would have to live with it.

Then her father had suddenly been summoned to the palace. Siegbo had looked at Ayoko, who was pouring millet and knew that, though she pretended to be concentrating on her household chores, she had missed nothing. Anoku had put on his outdoor osiba and hurried out to the King's palace. To the surprise of everybody in the priest's compound, Siegbo put on her own cloth, leaving her millet unpicked, and said she was going to the palace too.

One of the younger wives in the compound remarked under her breath, "Our chief wife is now a man, going to the palace, when the King wants our husband, the priest". She had said this looking in Ayoko's direction, but Ayoko simply looked away, as if she hadn't spoken. This was unusual for the sweet-talking Ayoko.

Her heart pounded fast, as if she'd been running, when her father walked slowly into the compound. She felt like running to him, telling him that it wasn't her fault, nor the fault of the women, but Fate, that had brought about this calamity.

When her mother appeared shortly after, she quickly followed her inside their dwelling. She didn't have long to wait.

Her mother told her that because Anoku had never liked the albinos, they were implying in the council that he must have known something about the albino's fate.

"But he didn't know anything about it, mother!" Ayoko cried.

"We all know that, even Iyalode, the priestess. But your father has allowed the suspicion of the people to get the better of him and said threatening things in the presence of that palace parrot, Mensa. So they've now asked your father to go and make a sacrifice for ten days to Ogene to find out from her the meaning of this."

Ayoko thought for a while and asked, "Mother, if I told them all that had happened, what would happen to me?"

"I don't know what they would do to you. But it would kill your father and myself, and even some members of the family. The kriors would weave our names into Shavi's history, and your father would be regarded as a false prophet of Ogene, who had to be punished through his daughter."

"Oh, mother, all I have caused you since the day of my birth is trouble."

"No, Ayoko, you have not. But sometimes I doubt very much if your father's prophecy and ambition for this family are not just too much."

"How, mother?"

"Oh, it's too deep for you to understand. Sometimes, I'm not so sure myself. Go and carry on with your house-work."

"Suppose they discover the albino. Won't he talk?"

"Ayoko, tomorrow is Ibu day, and nobody will go out to look for anyone. The day after, the men are going to meet those who went to the grazing ground beyond the hills, and when they start searching, Shoshovi is not going to tell them to go to Ime Oja hills, but to go to the other side first. By the time they discover him, he'll have long gone to his ancestors if

123

he has any, and people will think that he fell into a net set for
hyenas. We wrapped him securely in nets, you see.''

"A net for hyenas!" Ayoko repeated. So the women had
used their wire meat and fishing netting. But some of the
women had their own tags on their nets. Had they removed
their tags? How stupid could her mother and the others be? If
they found the albino's bones in twenty years' time, those tags
would still be there. Eventually the whole drama would surface like the body of a drowned man in the lake. And what
would happen to her family even then?

Their house was always full of roasted birds and fowls from
Ogene sacrifices. Mechanically, Ayoko packed many pieces of
cloth, took her mother's torch and knife, filled a leather bottle
with water and set out for the Ime Oja hills. She walked and
she walked, not thinking of fear. All she was thinking was
that, if any of them should be discovered, she didn't want
them to call her family murderers, or for the council of Elders
to condemn to death those women who had tried to help her.
She hadn't actually seen anyone killed in her life time, but she
had heard the kriors sing the dying song.

The cool bright night was on her side. She heard Ronje
before she saw him, as he started to shout and howl on seeing
her torch. His desperate voice fuelled her energy, and she ran.
By the time she reached him, he had become so exhausted that
all he could manage were pathetic grunts. She quickly cut the
wire and poured some water into his parched mouth, noticing
his body was full of sores. With frantic gestures she conveyed
to him the danger he was in. She told him to tie the cloth
around his body, and to go far, very far away. She ran a finger
across her throat dramatically, to show him that if he was
found, he would be killed.

Ronje soon got the message. He didn't know what to say to
her, and as for what to do, he was too numb to think. It felt as
if his body and his mind had stopped functioning. Ayoko left

him to his fate and ran for home. "At least, his blood is not on our hands," she thought.

16
Asogba Leaves Shavi

The Newark shivered from side to side. It taxied round the open space outside the high walls of Shavi and stopped, puffing up cloud and dust in its wake. This was greeted with controlled joy by Ista, Mendoza and Andria. The people of Shavi simply gazed in wonder. When Flip took the Newark up for a trial flight, and kept it in the air for five minutes, though a few of the Shavians still ran for cover, many, including the King, didn't run and hide. They only stood at a respectable distance from the vibrating plane. They did, however, allow their excitement to show. The albino people had done it, the bird of fire was flying again.

That the goddesses of the Ogene lakes had sent them, there was no doubt. Anoku, the chief priest, and his assistant Iyalode, had said that much. The people of Shavi worshipped birds and Ogene had sent them priests who looked like lepers to test their hospitality. "Wasn't it a good thing that I had the foresight to consult Ogene and come to the conclusion that they were not to be harmed or sent away?" Anoku asked anyone interested among the members of the council who stood there, watching in awe.

"Didn't I tell you that the bird would soon work and fly again? Didn't I say Ogene had told me that it would happen soon, and I stupidly thought that her 'soon' would be a hundred years or so. I didn't know Ogene was so impatient!"

Asogba saw his father nodding thoughtfully at the priest's claims. If he hadn't been the proper son of Patayon, he would have asked, "But look, Anoku, were you not the very person who told us a few months ago to be wary of the 'invaders'?" But that type of behaviour was not permitted. He wouldn't have won, anyway, because the people of Shavi knew that words were like rags – wherever you leave them, there they will stay. A few months before, the visitors had been like a new baby that arrived in their midst, unable to tell them what they had brought. Now they were beginning to show them that they could do much to make Shavi richer. Though Asogba had suspected that the bird of fire could fly, now that it had happened, he was dumbfounded.

Flip came out triumphant. He was relieved and happy, that special happiness and indescribable self-fulfilment that belongs to the creative scientist. There was no doubt about it, they could fly for at least five hours, and he was sure that whilst airborne, he would be able to get their bearings and would be picked up by western airport radar. God knew how he would connect and reply to them. But he calculated that they could fly low and land in any fairly large open field, since the Newark was a glider and capable of landing straight, helicopter-wise. As long as they didn't land on water or on houses, they would be safe. They would have to be very careful, very alert and trust to luck. But Flip knew that if he were at the controls, the danger would not be very great. With all that, he felt he deserved to be happy and allowed himself to be openly embraced and indulged by Ista and then by Andria.

"You've done it again!" Mendoza said appreciatively. All noticed that since Ronje's mysterious disappearance and, as a result of living with Ista, Mendoza had mellowed somewhat. He had stopped attacking and blaming Flip for everything. Flip had felt this change more than anybody else and liked it, because there was no need for the two of them to go on antagonising each other. So he replied modestly, "Oh, come off it, John. You know as well as I do that anybody can fly an aeroplane".

"With date oil?" laughed Mendoza. "Modesty is a lovely robe, but it ill-suits the likes of you, Flip."

And like two school boys, the men put their arms around each other, oblivious of the two very amused women trailing behind them.

"John, we've made it. We've perfected the impossible! This is the only plane I know that can fly on date oil."

"Highly refined date oil, for goodness sake. You two boys seem to have forgotten the amount of work we put in before we got that drop of oil," Ista reminded the rather over-enthusiastic scientists.

Mendoza stopped his his tracks and took his hand off Flip's shoulder. "I'm glad, really glad. I was beginning to worry about us in general, the children of course, but, in particular, these pregnant ladies. Now at least we have a choice, whether to stay or go."

"I want to leave as soon as possible. You know, it's not that the Shavians aren't friedly, it's just that they're not us," Andria observed.

Flip waited for Andria to catch up with him. "I know, I know. But I'd like to come back here and help." He shrugged his shoulders, "You know, come here with proper food and medicine – but especially food. So many people needn't die from the drought."

"And what are you going to use for money?" Mendoza asked.

"Well, those stones I found ages ago, I really don't know if they're worth anything, but if they are, the proceeds could go towards . . . "

"I'd forgotten all about them; you two keep secrets, don't you?" Mendoza started.

They couldn't continue their dialogue, as Asogba approached

with his usual wide grin and rickety gait, his arms outstretched in a congratulatory gesture.

"I go with you to your countirii," he said, laughing out loud at his ability to use the English Flip had been teaching him during their trips to the grazing lands and the cow market.

Ista laughed. "Oh, Flip, look – it's really true that the English-speaking race is so lingo-lazy that we impose it on others."

"Well, he wanted to learn, and I can't possibly teach him American or Yiddish. Did you hear what he's saying? He wants to come to our country. That'll pose a problem for me, since I have no country as such. Born and bred in Canada, trained in England, worked in America, now I sometimes feel I really belong nowhere," Flip said.

"Come to think of it, so are we all. But for the time being, England should be the 'countirii', so we'll set up from there," Mendoza said.

"And that'll be an even bigger problem for Asogba. He's black, he has no papers and he won't be well treated. I don't know. I'd rather not take him. Why does he want to go with us anyway? Is he no longer satisfied with worshipping the Ogene goddesses?"

"Oh dear, not again. We've unwittingly invaded the privacy of a people, and are about to rape her culture. I wonder what we're going to leave them with when we've finally finished with them. Will they still be the same, nice friendly people, after they've come to know the real us?" Andria asked despairingly.

But more obstacles were to be overcome before their departure. A big thing had happened in Shavi, a bird of fire had flown and soon the people who came in it would be leaving. That called for celebration. And at many celebrations in Shavi, the heroes were given new wives.

Ista and Andria found themselves helping to cook, sweating

129

in the heat once more. They couldn't complain about their delicate condition because women heavier than they were were busy heaving and stirring goats' meat and corn meal. They had started to sing the usual kora song, when suddenly one of the women cooking gave a cry of pain.

Shoshovi rushed to her, and with her deft fingers felt her bulging stomach. Her time was due. There was no doubt about it, the young woman was in labour.

Instinctively Ista washed her hands, and almost pushed past Shoshovi. "I am a doctor," she announced.

The other woman stared at her, nodded and smiled, and then pointed her back to meat roasting.

"That young woman needs my help, and I am a gynaecologist, not a meat roaster!" Ista cried. She went nearer to Shoshovi and started to gesticulate frantically, crying, "A woman doctor, that's me, can't you understand? That young woman needs my help!"

Three other women barred the door that led into what Ista suddenly realised was a kind of birth apartment. As the young woman's screams got louder and louder, Ista started to fret the more. It was a curious sight. One would have thought that it was Ista who was having the baby, and not the woman inside.

Andria for a while was at a loss what to do. "Leave them alone," she managed to say eventually. "Leave them to it, Ista."

Ista glared at her. "I'm a doctor. I was trained to save life, not to watch it being killed. Just look at what they are doing to the poor girl." Ista so much wanted to help.

The Shavi women had originally thought she wanted to watch a birth. Shoshovi tried to explain to Andria and Ista that this was a serious matter, not something for another woman to watch in fun. She gave up when she saw that Ista wasn't listening, and concentrated on the girl giving birth.

Ista and Andria looked on in helpless fascination as Shoshovi took a stool and sat down, her bended knee supporting the mother as she squatted, while another woman sat in front of the girl expectantly, ready to catch the child with her bare hands. The girl went on in agony for a long time until she was nearing exhaustion.

"Ah, it's a breach birth. She should have a Ceasarean."

Ista gestured with her hands again and used the few Shavian words she had mastered, but Shoshovi found whatever Ista wanted to say too distracting and she was jarring the rhythm with which the midwives were helping the girl so she persuaded her to go out of the room.

In despair Ista hurried to Flip. "I see what you mean," she cried. There are occasions when these people need our help badly. A woman is having a breach birth in there, very complicated, or it might even be a case of cord presentation, and they are making her squat and singing to her ... "

"Calm down Ista, I thought you believe in doing things like this the natural way. Can't you just watch and learn?"

"I do believe in the natural squatting birth or in whatever position the mother finds comfortable. But Flip this is a breach birth!" Ista shook her head vehemently. "Not a squatting position for a breach birth."

"Maybe they are used to squatting. Remember how Shoshovi cured Kisskiss simply by massage, when we all have almost given up hope about the child, but look at her now, she is as right as rain, isn't she?"

"Oh Flip, how can you be so callous? When it was your Newark, you were over the moon. A young girl may be dying over there in childbirth and all you can say is 'Maybe they are used to squatting'."

But it's true, isn't it? People squat here when they go to the lavatory, when cooking, and some of them squat when eating. And if this girl needs Ceasarean section, what chances are there of her surviving in a place like this anyway?"

131

"You mean I should leave it?"

"No for the sake of your peace of mind and your pride as a doctor, let's try to explain to them that maybe you can help."

"You know I can help. The trouble with you Flip is that you too want to leave them as untouched noble savages. Noble or not, they do need western ways sometimes, they do."

Flip smiled and said nothing, trying to remember the number of times Ista had vehemently defended Shavian culture. Maybe they were all hypocrites. Why couldn't they leave these people alone? They didn't ask for the Newark to crash among them.

Poor Ista struggled with herself, not knowing which way to turn. She regarded herself as a modern progressive doctor who kept an open mind on many issues, but now when confronted with something that went contrary to the grain of her western training, she found herself unable to cope.

When they got to the birth house, Flip was not allowed inside at all. Men who were standing some distance away told him that the birth of babies was the affair of women. The women helped each other, it had always been so, since Ogene, with the help of Olisa, created the earth, the hills, the sun and moon. If men went in there, they would only be intruding, and they did so only when there were no women around.

In despair, Ista left the men arguing and went back into the birth house. This time she was calm and docile.

She couldn't believe her eyes. The young mother was lying on a goatskin. Her still unwashed baby, wrapped in a new handwoven body cloth, was feeding contentedly at her breast, while the midwife was clearing away the afterbirth.

Ista's western arrogance had never suffered such a deflation. Dumbfounded, she crept up to her friend, Andria, and whispered, "How did it happen?"

"How did what happen? She gave birth to her child. This was a difficult one – a breach and rather exhausting, but oh,

Ista, it was so beautiful. The baby came out according to gravity, so the mother didn't have to bear down horizontally the way we do. The woman sitting behind her was to prevent her from having cramp. For a normal birth it would be just like going to the toilet.'' Andria's voice couldn't hide her enthusiasm.

"The baby's not damaged?"

"Well, look for yourself. He's suckling as thirstily as if he'd just arrived from a cattle farm."

"I wouldn't know. I haven't got a man who goes to cattle farms." Ista's voice was sharp. Andria stretched out her hand and took Ista's. "I'm sorry. I know how you must be feeling. I don't like it here very much, but sometimes when you're privileged to watch scenes like this, you wonder whether our complicated life is not just all our own making."

Ista stopped and looked directly into Andria's brown eyes. "Would you like a birth like this for the baby you're now carrying?"

"I don't know. I wouldn't mind, though not on such a dirty floor. It's beautiful to watch."

"Then you can't possibly know how I feel now. I admire these people, I love their way of life. What happened there was a simple proof of what their day-to-day life is like. And what did I do? I started to scream my arrogance at them, because still there inside me I feel that nothing that originates from Africa can ever stand up to our western ways. Can't you see, Andria, that I'm one of the greatest hypocrites alive?"

"Ista, I'm glad the Newark is rebuilt. This heartsearching can't be doing us much good. It's too disturbing."

"Why, because we're women who should be pampered?" Sarcasm was written all over Ista's face.

"Of course not!" Andria denied emphatically.

They walked away from the building. All the other women were excited by the arrival of the new baby. But they kept asking themselves: "What is the matter with the albino woman?

Why was she behaving oddly whilst another was giving birth?''
Some speculative ones said that maybe she was jealous, because
Dorf, who they thought was her child, must be over ten years
old. They all agreed, that must be it – maybe she was jealous,
wanting another child herself, and unable to have one. They all
shook their heads and some volunteered to make sacrifices to
Ogene on her behalf.

Meanwhile, the Prince of Shavi, Asogba the curious, was
busy convincing the council of Elders that he should be
allowed to go with the albinos. Mensa, the council's great
talker, asked, ''What will become of our prince if when he
gets there he becomes an albino himself? What will become of
the daughter of Anoku, who is betrothed to him?''

''Ogene has assured us that I won't become an albino, but
even if I do, my children will not,'' Asogba said in reply.

''But if these albinos came from Ogene, and the Ogene goddesses live in the land of the dead, is it right for our prince to go
there? Supposing they don't allow him to come back to us?
What I say is this, if our prince is bent on going, let us keep
one of the albino children, so if anything happens to him, we
can hold the albino child as ransom.''

''That would be all right if I was being forced to go. But,
my councillor, I'm going of my own free will. And who has
ever bargained with the Ogene before? I want to go with the
albino people, to learn their tricks. Then when I return I will
teach our young men to build and fly birds of fire. Now it takes
three trekking days to get to Ongar and sell our cattle. Then it
will take us only half a day, and with our bird of fire, I am
going to settle the Kokuma score. We will be the most respected and feared people of the desert. No longer will we be a
timid people hiding in a secluded oasis behind the Ogene
hills,'' Asogba's voice rang out, full of hope and ambition.

There was a sudden quiet after this, during which his words
sank in. The vision of Shavi thus conjured up was unthinkable,

but all could see that there was no immediate way of stopping him.

To settle the argument, Patayon coughed and said slowly, "I remember the day our visitors came, something rattled a warning sign in my old bones, telling me that things weren't going to be the same anymore. Our young people have seen the albinos and we can't tie a cloth over their eyes. If Asogba wants to go, let him. Nothing will happen to him, unless it has been ordained by Ogene. But before you do, young man, Ayoko must be prepared for you and you must make her a wife. Who knows, you may leave her with a child to look after when you go wandering with the albinos. Ayoko will have to be prepared with the other girls. Things have really changed." Patayon sighed deeply and then continued. "I hope Ogene will forgive our preparing the future Queen Mother of Shavi with other girls. But again this is a special case. The chief of the albinos and his assistant will be given new wives tonight to mark their great achievement. We still don't know what has happened to their third, the one with the eyes as blue as our lakes. But since we've searched high and low, and his body isn't found, maybe Ogene is keeping him somewhere. He may turn up by and by."

Presently, the first celebration of the bridal night started. It was different from the King's, for which the bride had long been prepared. The girls, Ayoko, Kito and Mope, were to be prepared tonight for marriage.

Flip, who was in a mood for celebration, was enjoying his barley beer drink and listening dreamily to the kora singer's monologue. It was enchanting, haunting music but Flip had by now heard it so many times that he could relegate it to an unobtrusive background sound as he enjoyed his drink with Mendoza and their new Shavian friends.

Many a time during the course of the evening, he noticed that his drinking friends were trying to convey something to him. He tried to follow their drift, but the round of Shavian wine made concentration impossible, so he waved off their gestures as the irrelevance of drinking behaviour. Nonetheless, he couldn't help but feel a kind of subtle conspiracy in the air.

No sooner had he relaxed and resigned himself for the evening than Mendoza nudged him, calling his attention to the girl, Kito, who was dancing invitingly towards him. He watched her, trying to lift his now heavy eyelids and smile at her politely as he thought was expected. But this ordinary action of his only raised an unnecessarily loud cheer from the onlookers. It was this cheer that made Flip muster some alertness. He sat up straight and refused any further drink.

People gestured him to step into the circle and dance with her. Then something clicked. He had heard that particular music before, he had seen someone invited into the ring to dance. Now he remembered, it was the King, the day of his bridal night. Was this girl going to be his bride? No, that would be too ridiculous. He looked at Mendoza, and saw that he too looked like someone in a coma. Flip had started to breathe heavily, when the girl vanished as suddenly as she had appeared.

Then, all in a moment, there was a scream that rent the atmosphere. Andria came over to Flip and asked, "What's happening to that girl?" "I've no idea," Flip murmured.

The music took on an intensive beat, and everybody seemed suddenly happy. A woman came out from the room which the girl had gone and waved her hands in the air ecstatically. She was greeted with cheers, and men pushed Flip back to the room he was sharing with Andria and Kisskiss.

It was then Asogba explained to him in his halting English, that Kito had been prepared for him.

"Tell them, I don't want a wife," Flip cried.

Asogba shook his head, trying to tell him that the Elders would be offended. That he and Mendoza had performed a great feat and that this was the way Shavi repaid her heroes.

"I don't want a wife. You've already married me off to Andria, I don't want a wife." For once Flip's cool seemed to be leaving him. He caught himself speaking in such a loud baying voice, that he was surprised at himself. He realised such an attitude wouldn't help him. Allowing his voice to sink to a confidential whisper, he asked whether the other girl was for Mendoza, and was not surprised when Asogba nodded.

As gently as they could, they made Asogba understand that, though they were grateful for the gift of the two beautiful women, they might be leaving Shavi forever.

"But they've been prepared. They've been clitorised. Only girls about to be married have this operation. It's too late to go back. You have to accept the wives. Even my Ayoko is being prepared tonight because I have to make her a wife, before I can fly away with you."

"Oh, my God, oh my God", Andria repeated, as she started to shake.

Their own argument stopped as a bigger one seemed to be coming from the gathering in the palace. The voice was Shoshovi's. She was shouting and from where they stood, she must be very angry.

Asogba was forced to leave his friends and their new wives to run down to the palace. Impulsively, Flip and Mendoza went with him, leaving the very sore girls lying on goatskins in the centre of their rooms.

"I'm going to clitorise my son's wife. Nobody else is going to do it. She's the future queen and I won't have any midwife messing about with her."

"But why? All the girls in Shavi are done by the midwife."

"I'm the Queen Mother, and I don't have to give explanations for the things I do".

Siegbo and her daughter stood by, watching and praying that the men wouldn't overrule Shoshovi. The midwife would say that Ayoko wasn't a virgin and they would be forced to disclose what had happened to Ronje. As the argument became heated, Iyalode the female priestess said, "Any mother can perform this operation. Shoshovi wants to do it for her future daughter. So what's the argument? Let her do it. What has it got to do with you men anyway? We don't interfere with your circumcision when you take the boys into the bush. So why can't you leave us alone? That part is our sex organ, so why should it be your problem?"

The men started to murmur, which was the break Shoshovi needed. She took Ayoko, who was now shivering as if from cold, into the inner room. Soon the operation was performed.

But instead of coming out into the circle to raise her arms to declare Ayoko a virgin as all were expecting, Shoshovi called in Siegbo and said sadly, "Siegbo my friend. I am very sorry. My son cannot marry your daughter, at least not yet. She has this swelling thing, look, all red and bloody. It is a strange disease. I think she must have caught it from the albino. Maybe your husband was right, if the albinos are carriers of disease. They must go and they must go tonight."

On hearing the news, the men were instantly carried away with hysteria. No one had time to ask how Ayoko had caught the disease. The fear that it could spread fired Anoku's imagination. "I said it, I said it," he went about saying, his hands on his head. Flip, not really knowing the details of what had happened, or what was about to happen to them, simply knew that they must leave. And as if to confirm his suspicion, Asogba slithered over to him and said urgently, "Flip, you must go now."

So, without saying proper farewells, as they had intended, they forced the Newark to lift them up out of Shavi. They had all been rather uneasy since Ronje's disappearance, and the hysteria of this night showed them that anything could happen, simply because they didn't understand each other. There was now no time to look for him. The plane worked, and that was a relief.

Sometime after take-off, Ista came screaming from the toilet, with the news that there was something there, something huge, black and formidable.

Mendoza grabbed his gun and was ready to shoot, when out came a young man he didn't very much like – Asogba.

"We have a problem," Mendoza breathed to Flip, "we're taking the Shavian prince with us to England, and we can't go back as we're running short of fuel".

All eyes turned to the grinning Asogba, his rickety bandy legs sticking out ridiculously of the goatskins in which he was covered.

"Who told him our country was colder? He's got goatskins on instead of his usual cloths!"

Flip sighed. "I'm afraid I'm guilty. I've been telling him how beautiful our life is. He wants to see it for himself".

17
Flip's Conscience

The Newark looked like a tiny bird in the sky, when first the people in Hebden Bridge in Yorkshire, England saw it. It was still autumn, and the crew could see the different shades of autumn browns, with the greenness of England permeating through. From the air they could see the gentle rise and fall of the hills and as they came nearer to the ground, a small brook working itself in and out of the grey rocks. There was peace, a cool English peace. But despite all this, the landscape was like a painting on a canvas. "At least we're not landing on a house," Flip remarked.

"I'm sure we're in England," said Mendoza, reassuringly.

"Just tell them to fasten themselves up. We're not landing in an airfield, as we have no means of answering them from the different aerodromes. I don't know what part of England this is, but you're right, it is England."

The Newark landed gently, not in the nosedive Flip had feared. Farmers left their animals and fields and ran to them, wanting to know whether they were hurt. One of the men who came was a clergyman, wearing his ecclesiastical air, ready to pronounce the last rites, but none of it was necessary.

"Yes, we lost our way. We'll be reporting it to the authorities". Flip tried very hard to ward off questions about Asogba, who now looked completely out of place and ludicrous in his make-shift goatskin shirt, and cloth tied around him to protect him from the autumn cold. He was visibly shaking, and clung to Flip almost childlike. People looked at him and thought, "Where did they get that tall black man from? Is he their servant or something, or is he their fool?" Typically of the English, they didn't say it aloud, but their gestures and stares said it all. Asogba felt like someone afflicted. An inferior mug of coffee was given to him. They spoke loudly to him as if he was not only deaf but demented, and his shivering body didn't help matters. He became a spectacle, almost non-human, a curiosity piece.

Asogba now started to have misgivings about his audacity. "Father told me not to come. He said, 'If you go to places where people have never been before, you'll see things which people have never seen before. The women say that Ayoko has caught a disease from these people. We don't know how she caught it. And you still want to go. Suppose you catch the disease yourself?'"

Asogba had said, "Yes, father, but my mind is made up. I must go."

"I'm ordering you as King not to leave this place with the albino people."

"You said yourself, father, that since they came here things have changed. No king's son has ever dared disobey his reigning father. This is one of the few offences punishable by death. If you tell the council that I have disobeyed you, they may order me to be exiled even though we're known to be gentle people. Why don't you just pretend you want me to go, so that you won't have to lose me. Suppose it all works out father? Think of our future, the future of Shavi. We will be great and powerful."

"I don't think we particularly want to be that powerful," Patayon had said.

"You're not going to reign forever, father. When I reign, I want us to be powerful. I'm talking about our future, not our past."

141

Father and son had left the argument like that, suspended, until the chaos about Ayoko forced him to hide in the Newark, determined to go with the albinos. Now he didn't know whether his father hadn't been right.

A policeman came up to him, and tried to conduct him away.

"Come, Mister," the man said, urging him along, none too gently.

"He's not a Mister, he's a prince," Ista protested, as she saw the way the officer was marching Asogba away.

"A prince indeed, so what am I, Maggie Thatcher?" The officer bayed, laughing.

"Flip must hurry up and get Asogba some papers. Otherwise he's going to be very unhappy in custody."

"Poor soul, we told him not to come, but he had to go and hide inside the Newark, so the fault is entirely his."

"It's too late now, Mendoza, to blame anybody. The fault is ours," Ista snapped.

"But how? And, by the way, are we still married?" Mendoza asked, jokingly.

"That little affair in Shavi was rather touching, but I'm still thinking about it."

Andria started to giggle. "I think I'll marry Flip if he asks me. Trouble is, I don't know if he's the marrying type. With him, one must be prepared to take second place to his profession."

"You won't have any trouble now on that score, they may not take him back. He left the sinking boat," Mendoza predicted.

"But what I want to know is this. Where's that urgency that pushed us into leaving Europe in the first place? Look at the papers on that table. All I can see is elections and political news. Nothing is being written about the nuclear war," Ista commented.

"I know how you feel. Sometimes it makes me think that I'm already dead and that we're all in heaven or hell or wherever the likes of us go. One minute it was holocaust, the next, people behave as if nothing's happened at all. It's ridiculous. It makes me feel ashamed."

Flip soon came back with piles of clothes, papers and news. "The immigration officials are looking with interest into our story. Story, they called it. Then I got the big man, and he's now testifying to our sanity. Do you know that they didn't blow Europe up?"

"We were just talking about it," Andria said.

"I keep telling people that there is a big Man or Woman up there, who is watching everything with amusement. He just wouldn't let us tiny creatures blow up this wonderful earth He/She has created. Because by human calculations all was ready to go up in smoke three months ago."

"Some woman, Maria Theresa or somebody, invited both parties to meet, and each party talked itself dry, and then she prayed for the world, and said, go back to the United Nations and start all over again. In fact I think they're still talking. But for the first time, the tragedy of it struck home."

"Just like that?" Ista exclaimed.

"Just like that, and because of it we've been to a place like Shavi and disrupted their tranquil life. Is Asogba still sleeping? I've brought him more suitable clothes."

"No, the immigration officials have come for him. They'll keep him for a few days before they let him out. They're taking him to Pentonville Prison."

"Huh, what a welcome! Well, I'll have to go back to London on the afternoon train. And I'm going to Clerkenwell to show the Shavi stones to someone. If they're worth anything, we'll have to meet again and share the money or, as I'd prefer, use it to send drought relief to Shavi."

"I wouldn't mind going back, to help the women," Ista said.

"But, er . . . Aren't you going into hospital, you know the baby . . . ''

Ista started to smile. The sophisticated doctor, the woman with a brain, was coming back. "No," she shook her now unpinned hair, shaggy from the trimming she had given it with the sharp knives the women of Shavi used for trimming feathers. "No," she repeated dramatically. "I'm not having the baby."

"Oh, I'm sorry . . . I think it would have been fun, you know, you and Mendoza, the new baby and Dorf," Flip said, pulling hard at his red beard.

"You know, Flip, one day you're going to pull that beard off," Andria said in a brave effort to hide Flip's confusion.

Flip was the kind of person to whom one and one must always be two. He now looked confused, helpless and childlike. To him, since Mendoza and Ista had been happy in Shavi, why should they not continue to be so in Europe?

Absentmindedly he took Andria's hand and said slowly, "We're having ours. And because of that I'm going back to the Research Institute. I'm taking my job back. And you, Mendoza, are you doing the same, going back to work?"

"I'm not as hot a commodity as you are, and I resigned with a big row. I'd like to see how much we make from those stones."

"Ah, Mendoza, please don't bank too much on the stones. In the next few months Shavi will be facing another drought. The food was already running out before we left and there's not going to be any rain for the next six months. So if we can, we must send them a planeload of rice and beans and corn, because they'll need it. I hope we can teach their prince the use of modern farming techniques, because I'm sure we have a lot to learn from them in return."

"They have their stones, which you won't reveal the source of. But I'm sure you got them during one of your trips with

Asogba. Very unsporting of you to keep it all to youself. If they're worth a lot of money, then, Philip Wagner, only earthquakes will stop me from going back,'' Mendoza said seriously.

"Look, Mendoza, you're much more English than any of us. Your mother was a lady, your father, whose ancestors were both Jewish and Spanish, was a product of Eton. You know and I know if I reveal that what will happen to the Shavian culture. You know it'll be eroded, their whole way of life will disappear. You see, when we came to them, they placed us in their best house. Their prince is now here with us, and we're being told that he hasn't been immunised, that because he's black and in strange clothes, he has to be put in jail. Because that's where they're taking him. Do you want the Shavians to be exactly like us? I hope the stones are worthless, I really do hope so. I only had to tell you at all in case they're of any value. Meanwhile, I think we should try and get Asogba free, expose him to our farming methods, and maybe make him a good friend. That way, we'll be able to repay their hospitality.''

''Flip, one thing that has always made me mad at you is the way you think you can play God. Remember you almost got us all killed,'' said Mendoza.

And there they left the conversation.

Two days later, Andria and Flip got married in London, with a small reception in the evening at the Mall. Mendoza came, though Ista couldn't as she was very soon to go into hospital to abort her baby, and everybody knew that she didn't want to see Mendoza. More people than expected turned up, because Flip, in his simple way, was well liked.

Journalists and photographers swarmed around them wanting the full story of how they landed in Shavi. None of the party wanted the story revealed, but bits and pieces were being put together by the curious media.

"Pity Asogba couldn't be here with us,'' Andria said wistfully.

"Shame, isn't it? I've been following his movements over the phone. They're transferring him to Pentonville open prison tomorrow. I still have to convince immigration that he wasn't purposely illegal and that he'll go home as soon as we're settled. I told them to treat him well."

"I hope so. Immigration officers can be really something."

"Well, as I said earlier, he'll soon be in an open prison. Maybe it's better for him in a way, because he still jumps at the sight of motor cars. He needs to be settled and calmed. Poor man, he looks so bewildered. A farm in Lowestoft is willing to take him on as a farm labourer, and he'll be at home with the English cattle. I must try and see him before we leave for our very, very short honeymoon," Flip concluded, encircling Andria's bulging waist with his arm.

Flip had time to talk to Mendoza about the stones. Yes, they were valuable, very hard, almost like diamonds, and the few pieces he had brought would make them all richer by a couple of thousand pounds each. He was going to use part of the money to send aid to the people of Shavi and also to train some of the people in modern agricultural methods.

"But they'll have to be adapted to the desert conditions, won't they?" Andria asked.

"Yes, of course, although I'm leaving the whole project with the experts. I may not have time to supervise the plan myself, but I have one or two very reliable people in mind," Flip said confidently.

Asogba didn't stay long in prison, yet he was still bewildered about the pace of life, and the fact that there were so many albino people. He noticed that he no longer saw his friends from Shavi. They had handed him over to other white people. He had stopped calling them "albino" because he met many people who came from his part of the world and also many from the Caribbean in the prison. He had started calling them whites or Charlies. And with the few English words he mastered, he now knew that they were not gods at all. They were people, and they treated people of different skin colour as if they were afflicted.

As the months rolled by, the pressures on Flip built up. He decided he would have to entrust the collecting of the Shavi stones to a company, which would take care of the Shavian people's welfare. He became almost helpless when Mendoza said that he would head such a company, because he needed a break from his scientific career. He wanted a little adventure also.

"You really don't need to go out there, Flip. Think of Andria and her condition," Mendoza pointed out. "And don't forget that Asogba now speaks a bit of English. If we don't make use of those stones now, who is to stop him selling the collecting rights to the French?"

So, to quieten his nagging conscience, Flip decided that it would be better for them to ask Asogba himself. Flip definitely couldn't go back to Shavi as he was too busy. His talent was needed at the Research Institute. The arms race had taken a new turn. The powers had by then decided that, instead of building more nuclear arms, they would perfect the conventional ones. Flip was needed to think out ways of making deadlier conventional weapons from the nuclear pile up. He was again enthusiastic about this and would talk of nothing else. The people of Shavi – well, that episode had been an adventure. But, on Andria's insistence, he would do whatever Asogba wanted for his people. They arranged to meet Asogba at the farm, where he was fast learning modern agricultural methods.

Flip hardly recognised Asogba in his grey wool dungarees and felt hat. He still had his magnificent look, but his usually bare legs were now covered, and somehow it didn't quite suit his bandy legs. He welcomed them effusively, and again Flip felt a sense of misgiving.

147

The village inn where Flip and Mendoza took Asogba to eat was panelled in dark oak. Its dark interior was reminiscent of the dome houses of Shavi. Asogba was fed on ploughman's lunch, as he still liked to chew tough and crusty food. Then he drank a great quantity of beer.

"What would you like to have for Shavi?" Mendoza started on the subject without meandering.

Before Flip could protest, Asogba went on to enumerate all he wanted. "I like to take farm jeep, motor car to bore water holes, motor cars to travel to cattle market and the valley of the shepherds. I like two guns to kill hyenas and other animals for food."

"Well, his demands are modest, aren't they?" Mendoza said rapidly in English, to the now confused Flip.

"How did he know he's entitled to all these, Mendoza? Have you been visiting Asogba behind my back?" Flip asked, disguising his anger.

"Well, come on, old chap. We landed in Shavi together. I had to come and see that he was well looked after. You were away on your honeymoon, and now you're immersed in your work. The man wants a motor car, to show off to his people. So what's wrong with that?"

Slowly and with patience, Flip explained to Asogba that the West would be buying the Shavi stones and, that in return, they would be given plenty of different foods to supplement their diet, especially during droughts.

Asogba's face lit up at this. "Yes, you people have more food than you need. I see vegetables thrown into the fields. I see good meat thrown away. We need them. You can never run out of food. Our people will not need to work for food again. They'll search, dig and collect Shavi stones for you."

Flip coughed to call attention to the fact that he wanted to say something to the contrary. "When Mendoza has seen to it that you have more water holes, that will help you to grow more food as well."

Asogba threw his head to one side, the way he had seen the white men do when they were thinking, and screwed up his face. He had learnt from the blacks he met in prison that this was a society in which it was not always right to say what one thinks. He knew what he wanted for his people. He wanted his people to be as great as these white people. But Flip would never understand. So he gave his lopsided grin once more and agreed. "Yes, we will concentrate on boring water holes."

With that they left Asogba on the farm. He stood there awkwardly in his wellingtons, wearing his dungarees and felt hat, waving and admiring Flip's new Rover. He must go back to Shavi with one of those. Mendoza had told him that with the Shavi stones, his people could have anything they wanted.

When he walked back to the cottage in which he lived, he wondered what these white people wanted with the Shavi stones. He knew that there were many in Shavi, scattered all over the place. But he was going to make sure that no white man would be allowed to pick one by himself. That way he was going to make them work for him.

"Shavi will be great, and I will inherit a great people, not cattle rearers or water hole diggers."

Asogba made sure that in the next few days, he persuaded the farmer to teach him how to drive. The farmer readily obliged, as he had been instructed to humour the prince of Shavi. As soon as Asogba could start and reverse a car, he was impatient to go back to Shavi.

18
Changed Asogba

The gods couldn't have been kinder to the albino people the day a small aircraft landed again in Shavi.

It was in the middle of another drought. The Ogene lakes, which were full of water when John Mendoza, Flip, Andria, Ista and the children landed there, had now dried almost to a trickle, so full of muddy salt that it was undrinkable. The people seemed to have shrivelled with the dryness and all vegetation had gone deep brown as if roasted.

The Shavians, who had been waiting for the arrival of their prince, all these months, knew as soon as they saw the blob in the sky that Asogba was back. This time, Mendoza, who commanded the trip, had made sure they got there in the morning, when he calculated that it would be cooler. He was right, but it was a kind of coolness he hadn't counted on – the harmattan dry coolness.

To Asogba everything seemed to have shrunk. The large foot track he had dreamt of when he was in Pentonville prison seemed now to have lost some of its largeness. The Shavians ran out with delight, as Asogba had expected. The women, their cloths flying in the wind, screamed with sheer joy and hope when they saw Asogba coming out with more and more albinos. The palace guards, who had been trained to be fast runners, reached him first.

"You have grown fat, our prince. What did Ogene feed you with up there in the sky?" one of the guards cried.

"Ogene? Oh yes, Ogene!" Then Asogba laughed, a chill diplomatic laugh that did not ring true to his own ears, to say nothing of the palace guards who stood by, looking confused and embarrassed. Asogba seemed faintly patronising. Even his walk was different. Why, for example, did he put his hands on his hips, why did he have to throw his head back when he emitted his new empty laugh and why did he preface every speech by making a fist of one of his hands, placing it before his mouth, and letting out a cough that was as empty as his laughter? He exchanged more impersonal greetings with many of his old friends, shaking their hands instead of embracing them. His coldness was especially noticeable as many of them came tearing over the rocks with the cloth flying, shouting, with their arms held wide in welcome. When Asogba turned round to them and shook their hands, the exuberance was instantly controlled, hitherto happy relatives were reduced to apologising for their happiness.

Before long, Asogba asked, "My father, the King. Is he well?"

There seemed to go through the little crowd now assembled a kind of indescribable relief that Asogba could remember such an ordinary person as his father.

"He is well and he is not so well. The drought, you see, many animals have died. We haven't had rain for eight months, even though we've been making sacrifices to Ogene," said a youth standing by, keen to acquaint Asogba with all their calamities.

"Our prayers have been answered, now that Ogene has sent you back. Somehow I know that things will be alright."

"Heh, don't I recognise that voice? Aren't you one of the boys from the household of Anoku the priest?" Here Asogba grinned with the near abandon of his old self. "And Ayoko, is she well?"

"Shame has killed Anoku. He died soon after your mother said you would not be marrying Ayoko, since Anoku had said that Ogene destined her from birth to be your wife. His death was sudden. The palace stopped sending food to his household, and then the drought started, and Anoku started to pray by the Ogene lakes every day. One minute he was praying, the next he was dead," a young woman explained.

"But, Ayoko, is she well now?" Asogba asked seriously, directing his gaze to the boy from Anoku's household.

"She is well and she is not well," the boy replied, doubtfully.

Asogba knew that he had to be satisfied with that indefinite answer until he had seen Ayoko himself. Meanwhile he had many things he wanted to do. He walked away from the now curious group. After a few rather exaggerated strides, he turned abruptly and warned, "No one should talk to the albinos. They carry weapons of death in their speech and in their bodies. They're not the friends we think they are. They're dangerous. Anyone, I repeat, anyone found talking with any of them will receive this." Here Asogba brought out a gun, and shot a heap of dry twigs which instantly began to burn.

The Shavians watching him recoiled in horror. Asogba had changed. They went back quickly to tell what they had seen and heard to their different compounds. Mendoza and the men with him watched Asogba. Their practised eyes missed very little. "I suspected this. The fool is going to be difficult. I wish to God Flip had agreed to come with us, it would have saved us from having to amuse this character."

"Well, he's not been that bad considering that his stay in civilisation was only a year or so. He'll act to the pattern of most of them, another African leader drunk with power," replied Charles Fielding, who was John Mendoza's pilot.

Asogba was surprised to see the condition of his parents. They looked emaciated and weaker than he could ever remember. He was not aware that the drought affected the people of Shavi this much, because before he used to be one of them. Now he could see the situation with the eye of an outsider. Flip was right. Food was important to the people of Shavi, if they were to be strong and help him conquer the desert, which he hoped one day to do.

Not long after his arrival, Asogba, who now seemed to be taking over the ruling of Shavi without the permission of Patayon or the new priests or even the council, ordered everybody to swear that they wouldn't say a word to the albinos. Whenever they asked anything of anybody, the person should report it to the palace. "They are not good," Asogba thundered. "When I came to their country, they put me in prison, they called me black, just as we call them albinos. But they made it seem as if my blackness was a disease, akin to stupidity. They dehumanised me, as they do to some blacks who come from a place called the Caribbean. But I kept my sanity and dignity because I have Shavi as my prop and because I am an African. Do you all know why they are here? They took the trouble to bring me back, not because they like us or care for what happened to me. They are here because they want the Ogene stones from us. We have to use those stones to get food from them. They won't give us anything for nothing, which was why they didn't at first understand our kindness to them when they came here. If anyone or any family gives away the secrets of where the Ogene stones are to the albino people, that person will be killed with this." Again Asogba emphasised his seriousness by raising his new toy – the gun he was carrying – and pointing it at them. The palace men who had seen him use it in the morning cringed and quivered.

Patayon, who was already feeling better after being fed with pre-fluffed American rice, shook his head sadly and said, "I said, it didn't I, that the albinos would bring nothing but evil?

They have turned my son into a killer, who fears neither Ogene nor men.''

''Don't blame the albinos. Our prince wanted to go. This power is new to him. Let us just pray that he soon realises how power corrupts,'' Egbongbele said, cautiously.

''Well, let us hope it won't be too long before he changes,'' Patayon replied.

The people of Shavi swore not to reveal the secrets of the Shavi stones to the albinos. As Asogba was the only one who could understand English, he told Mendoza and his men that the first thing they needed, apart from food, was to instal machines that would bore more water holes. From what Asogba had seen in Europe, he knew that they were capable of doing this in no time.

Though the drought continued, and though many tribes of the desert died like locusts, the people of Shavi thrived. They now had water holes from which they could pump out water. It was so like a miracle to them that they dubbed this easy water, ''magic water''.

The Shavians didn't feel the drought any more. The older people got much better, children thrived and Asogba rode about in his new jeep, which was specially tropicalised for his desert home. He had wanted to go and show off his cars at the cattle market, but he later decided that there was no need for that, because he could see that his father worried over him.

''You're making other people jealous. If you share what you get with our people, they will pray for you,'' Patayon began out of the blue, when Asogba roared into the council one afternoon.

''Well, father, aren't I doing enough? Look at our place and look at our valley. This is the only place in this desert where you have constant water. Look at our women and see how clean they can afford to keep their body cloth. What else do you want me to do for our people, father? You've no idea what

I suffered from the albinos. And don't forget, that when I was determined to go with them, you and your council refused to give me permission . . . ''

"You cannot talk to us like that. Your father is still our King. He may not be able to speak the albino language or roar about creating dust in their land-boat, but he is still our King," Egbongbele's voice, though weak with age, rang out.

Mensa chimed in, "You'll be our King soon. Look at your father, he was ill when you returned, now the worry over you is making him worse. You know that the prince of any group of people in the desert looks after their animals, but when did you last visit the valley of the shepherds? How many cows have we now in Shavi? Tell me that, Asogba, the son of Patayon."

"I cannot tell you, Mensa the great talker. You're right, I haven't been to the cattle market, but if it's cows you want, you'll have cows," he laughed at his own joke. "A few years ago, you laughed at my mother for wanting a cow, and said that her greed was insatiable. I'll give you cows, Mensa. I'll go to the cattle market, don't you worry. I'll go there in style and then my people will be proud of me!"

Asogba was so incensed that he jumped into his car and roared out of the palace compound. He drove madly, straight to Mendoza, and bursting upon him with little ceremony, he bayed, "Mr Mendoza, you will have to go back to your country and bring me in less than a week two hundred guns and ammunition.''

"What are you going to use them for?" Mendoza asked, surprised at Asogba's hastiness.

"Look here, get me the guns or I'll stop giving you the Ogene stones!" Asogba stormed.

Mendoza didn't know how to reach this changed Asogba. He wished now he had listened to Flip. He wanted to make his pile and get out quickly. The stones weren't diamonds, or anything that precious, and though their toughness could make

155

them useful for industry, ten plane loads had already saturated the market. A demand hadn't really been created, but that was too complicated to explain to the power-drunk Asogba. He would comply this time, supply him with the guns he wanted, and make another trip to pay the men he had hired. He wanted to consolidate his profits quickly, and pull out, then if the stones proved industrially useful in the future, he would invest in them again. But for the moment he had to make a temporary stop.

How was he to explain all this to Asogba, who was already making wild plans? Well the Shavians should learn to do it the western way. After all, places like America and the United Kingdom didn't have to come to Shavi to learn their know-how. "We have modern technology, so they should learn from us. I've given them all the help I could. The more help we give, the more they wish to buy prestigious things like arms and ammunition, and now they no longer do their farming as vigorously as they used to when we first came here. Maybe it would be a blessing in disguise if I stopped after two or three more trips. They should learn to do things the western way."

With that, Mendoza felt he had acquitted himself of his Shavian responsibility.

19
Defeated Elders

If Asogba was causing Mendoza, Flip and the Elders of Shavi a great deal of worry, he was completely oblivious.

Soon, the practised noses of the Shavian farmers told them that another long and cruel drought was imminent. When one breathed in in the early morning, the sharp air grated through the nostrils, stinging the lungs. This air brought with it a nasty wind, that had collected a good pile of dust from the desert in its wake, and was so strong that not even the formidable hills surrounding Shavi could protect people, animals and plants from it. The Shavians knew, when they started having ashy faces, prematurely grey hairs and stinging noses, that another unkind and ugly drought was on its way.

Not that the drought was strange to Shavian farmers. They had had its like for many, many years, and regarded it as a test of strength. One was wont to hear a farmer brag to his lazy son, "I have lived and brought my family through six droughts. Can you bring a family through a drought?" This usually shamed an arrogant young man into silence so that he would stalk away.

At the onset of the signs of the approaching drought, the farmers, with the full blessing of the King's Elders, would work out a survival plan. The small and most vulnerable water holes would be protected. Some rich families would go out and buy a camel, so that they could rely on its capacity to keep water as a last resort. If all else failed, they would eat the meat, and survive for weeks on the blood collected at its death. Others would collect millet and barley twigs for their animals, and keep the dung for manure and lining the tops of their pagoda-like roofs. At the same time, they would preserve as much grain as possible. A few people habitually died, but not more than in cold countries during a bitter and unkind winter. The more prepared people were, the less they were affected. Being in the shadow of hills, the Shavians were much better protected than most of their nomadic neighbours.

The council of Elders noticed the changing wind and began to plan a detailed survival programme. Mensa, the councillor who was so good at saying the obvious and who always felt that if he didn't say anything, people would think that he had little knowledge, now got up, and saluted the King and the Elders. "We know that a drought is imminent, King and Elders. But this time there is no need for us to start making elaborate plans. What we have to do is to get more birds with which to thank the goddess of Ogene, so that she will send us more and more of those food-bearing birds driven by the albinos. We can get all the food we need from them. We have been fortunate so far, and I don't see why we should go on working in this biting wind. When I woke this morning the wind stung my eyes and nostrils ... "

King Patayon quickly interrupted, as he could sense the oncoming of one of Mensa's endless tirades. His council was noted for patience and longsuffering, but the winds were changing fast, and this was one of those few occasions when quick decisions followed by equally swift action were called for. Patayon coughed, and thanked his "able" councillor Mensa. But he reminded him that Shavi must never forget what she stands for. "We stand for independence, we stand for freedom. If we allow ourselves to be completely dependent on the albinos, and don't prepare ourselves for the worst, I hate to think what will happen to us if for any reason they fail to bring food.''

Normally, after a weighty comment like this one, the council of Elders would allow a few minutes to pass before replying to the King. It was a mark of respect, and also gave council members time to think carefully about their reply.

But Asogba did not allow any time to elapse before he started with, ''But, father, the albinos can never fail. I have been to their country. They have hundreds and hundreds of birds of fire that swoop and fly over their countries and villages like vultures at play. They have heaps and heaps of food, so that they can never eat all they produce. There, people even starve themselves to look good. They think it is bad to eat well, so they throw away the good food they produce. So you see that they don't know all as we think they do. As long as we supply them with Ogene stones, they'll send us more food than we'll ever need. They promised me this. All they have to do to see us through a bad patch is to send us two or three birds of fire loaded with food once or twice a month.''

These days, when Asogba spoke in this vein, the council members were always silent. Many of them were still confused as to the status of the albinos. Were they the messengers of Ogene or were they just ordinary people who happened to live in the sky? Most believed the latter. Asogba had tried to explain that the plane that took him away came down on land when they arrived at their destination – the albinos' country. But the Shavians could never imagine such a thing, so Asogba had let them be. He and many of his age group knew the facts, and as far as he was concerned, that was all that mattered.

At length, Egbongbele asked, ''Our Prince, do you see a time when we won't need to farm at all, and the goddess will go on sending food?''

The question was meant to be cynical, but if Asogba had heard the cynical note, he acted as if he hadn't. In fact, he deliberately took Egbongbele literally, though so naturally that his listeners couldn't tell whether it was by design or accident. He stood, and began to talk excitedly of his dream. "Yes, our Wise One, that we are the chosen people of the desert, there is no doubt. That was why Ogene singled us out for a special visitation of the albino people. How can our goddess fail us when she herself watched our creation? Has the rain ever failed to fall when Ogene ordered it to? Or has the day ever failed to bring sunlight or the night darkness? If all these things happen without our worrying over them, how then do you think Ogene can fail to bring birds of fire to feed our miserable selves? All we have to do is to let her ministers know. The albino, Mendoza, comes often now. If he can't come, Ogene will send somebody else. There are millions and millions of albinos. So, my Wise One, there is going to be a time when we won't have to work on our farms, and what's more, that time is coming soon." Asogba's smile was so fatuous that for the first time, the old man resented the previously respected title, "Wise One".

Patayon sensed his friend's embarrassment and came to his rescue. "It would still be wiser to prepare ourselves for a bad drought. There is a sense of celebration for the achievement when we have survived one. History is made. We have a landmark for the passage of time. What will we do if we stop working for the food we eat and the cloth we use in covering our nakedness? We will be less human. There won't be any need to celebrate anything, because the joy of providing for ourselves will have been taken from us."

"You mean, my father and King, that you want to celebrate each drought with new wives? Asogba's lopsided grin was as bland as ever.

There was suppressed laughter from the younger side of the council. Everyone present knew that that was not what Patayon had meant, but Asogba was bent on trivialising the feelings of the older ones. Many of them felt for Patayon. Fate had really dealt unfairly with the "Slow One" when he sent this arrogant prince to be his son. It would have been bearable if Patayon had been a bad king. But for a good king to have a son like this was one of those intricate ironies of fate which no-one could unravel.

"People in the desert call us the shy ones ruled by the Slow One. All this is going to change, because Ogene wills it. We're no longer going to be called the shy ones. Why should we be shy? We are a strong tribe, good hard-working people. And why should our ruler be called "the Slow One"? Are these flattering titles?"

A unanimous "No" came from the corner reserved for the younger men.

"Mendoza will bring loads of food, peanuts, rice, medicines called pills that you swallow and don't have to drink, that cure you without being bitter. Ogene has sent us all this, and you want us to throw it all away. If we do, I know that she will take her bounty elsewhere. We may be her only worshippers in these parts, but we're not the only people living in this area. Please, our Elders, do remember that. As for work to occupy us, we have much more important things to do. 'Shame,' you Elders tell us, 'kills faster than disease'. But we have been living in shame behind these hills for generations. Now there are going to be changes. We're no longer going to live in shame. The desert is going to know that the people of Shavi are great. Is that not so?"

"It is very much so."

To the amazement of the Elders, shouts of bravado burst out from about half the council, mainly the younger men. Asogba himself had been so carried away by his own vision and eloquence, that when the shout of admiration came, he almost staggered. He hadn't realised the power of his own words, forgetting that words are like rags, according to the old proverb.

Nonetheless, he collected himself and smiled, this time genuinely.

He knew that in a few days, Mendoza would be coming to Shavi with the guns and food he had ordered. He had given him a larger than average bag of Ogene stones. He knew that there would be famine, so he had rationed the stones in such a way that food would forever be coming to Shavi. Sometimes he worried lest they run out of stones; what could the Shavians contribute to the world then? He could find no answer to this irritating question. The more difficult he found it, the angrier he got with his father and the Elders sitting in council and talking banalties all day long, feeling smug and secure behind the Shavi hills. "Why are we so behind other people?" he asked. "It must be because of our isolation."

The only thing he could do now was to train his men to use guns so that they would have the confidence to go out beyond their hills and see whether they too could have a say in the world around them. Hadn't he been told that this was how England's Empire was established? He and his men would start their expansion likewise. Once they had expanded beyond their hills, they would have more cattle and be able to trade in camels as well. Their neighbours looked down on them because they bred cattle which were used only for bride prices and for beef, and prided themselves on rearing camels, the princely trade of the desert, where camels are indispensable. They had hidden behind the hills for too long. They were no longer true nomads, neither were they true cattle farmers, and this had put them at the mercy of any minor drought. He was going to alter all that.

Although these thoughts had been going through his head since his arrival from Europe, he couldn't discuss them with anyone. His younger brother, Viyon, regarded him as a hero, with vast knowledge of the world. But they were not of the same mother. Viyon's mother and his own were not very kind towards one another. If the women could have afforded to be open enemies, they would have been, but that wasn't allowed in the palace of the King. So they both avoided each other as much as possible, though Viyon adored and worshipped his big brother.

Sometimes, though, Asogba would relent and tell him his dreams, based on some of the things he had seen in Europe. He had long convinced him that the albinos weren't gods, but in fact wicked people, who threw him into prison simply because he was black. But he didn't let that worry him much, what he wanted was a little of their riches and their way of life. "They live well, too well, Viyon, those albino people."

"What goddess do they make sacrifice to? She must be powerful," Viyon would ask.

"I don't think they worship anything much. Some of them go to big buildings on special days and worship some person they say is the son of the Almighty God."

"I know, like the Moslems in the cattle market at Ongar?"

"Hmm, something like that. They have different names for their Son of God."

"So how many gods do they have?"

"I don't know. Sometimes they say He is one, at other times they say He is three. But if you asked me, I'd say that they don't fear any god or goddess. They behave as if they have no tomorrow. People get killed and beaten up by their guards, but I didn't fear them, because I knew I'd my Shavi to come back to."

Viyon would open his eyes wide, beat one fisted hand into the other, and shout, "The Ongar people will call us the bold people of Shavi".

And sometimes when they were both carried away they would declare that they would seek out the kingdom of the Kokumas and enslave them the way they had enslaved their ancestors, because anything is possible to the man with a killing weapon, who flies like a bird in the sky.

The meeting of the council today was timely. It was giving Asogba the opportunity to acquaint the Elders with part of his grand plan which they had not known of before.

"And if we don't farm any longer, what shall we do then?" Patayon asked once more, in a shaky, despairing voice.

"We shall expand. We shall let our neighbours know of our existence. We shall let them know that the Shavians are great. We shall let the Kokumas know that we are still very much alive."

"How are you going to achieve all this, young man?" Egbongbele asked, shaking his silvery head.

"That's not for you to think about, Wise One. I'll think about all that, and the new blood of Shavi will help me in the carriage of my plans." Asogba's voice was now becoming loud as though he were giving orders. He looked tall and confident, so that even his bandy legs seemed almost straight.

Again Asogba was cheered. Egbongbele turned and looked slowly at his friend of many years, and they both sighed. Neither of them wished to display their innocence and stupidity by asking any more questions. But their silent look said it all: "Have we lived beyond our time?"

When, a few days later, the krior announcers of Shavi called all men to get up from their sleeping places and go with the Prince beyond the hills, Patayon, Egbongbele and the other elderly advisers asked again, "Have we lived beyond our years?"

As they couldn't find the answer, they took refuge in deeper silence.

As for Asogbe, he had started to train his Shavian desert army.

20
Ista

The sounds of a robin woke Ista up early. She had wanted to stay longer in bed. In was damp, grey and cloudy, but all this didn't deter the robin that seemed to have made the window onto the garden its home. Who could blame it? It was early May, and the sun should be shining, but in Colswold, where her mother's cottage always gave her refuge when she needed it, it was still cold and wintry.

Neighbours had asked her to sell the cottage, but she had refused, as she wanted to keep it for sentimental reasons. She wanted a place she could really regard as her home. She had done a great deal of travelling in the past years, but always came back to Colswold to see her mother and her aunt Dorothy who had decided to bury themselves there. Not that she had grown up there. On the contrary, she and her parents had lived in the smartest part of London's Kentish Town. She had gone to Camden School for Girls, but had to change when her father, a doctor like herself, decided to go to Yemen for a couple of years. She'd then gone to an elite boarding school in Great Malvern. She saw her father only once after her admission to Charing Cross Hospital as a medical student. He died when she was still in her first year which was when aunt Dorothy had taken over. She had found this quiet place where there was no other connection with the city, except the railway line to London. It was an ideal place. For the last ten years she had always come here whenever she had a break or, like now, when she wanted a refuge. The difference now was that her mother was dead too. She had died just before Ista had taken off with Mendoza and the others.

The robin was still twittering and hopping about its nest. Ista wondered why it was restless so early in the morning. She was restless too. She smiled sardonically now at the recollection of the past months: Andria and Flip getting married, and on the spur of the moment John asking her to marry him since she too was carrying a child. Andria was delighted to be married to Flip, who was steady, a little over romantic, but a nice man. And Mendoza? Living with Mendoza would be like living with a hurricane. No-one could tell when it would rise, strike and demolish. But why had she not at least kept the child?

Now that was the question that was making her restless. She had checked in at a clinic and funnily enough caught herself telling the staff that she was Mrs. John Mendoza. She'd said she wanted the abortion because she had had four children, and didn't want any more. The staff and nurses had believed her. They didn't ask any questions, but she noticed that a woman down the corridor who had lost a baby she badly wanted received conspicuously more attention and sympathy than she did. The woman knew about her. They must have told her that she was aborting her child. They had met once on the corridor, and the woman had given her a look which said, "You murderer. How can you kill your own child?"

In reply, Ista had given the woman a clumsy, rather uncertain smile. But she didn't smile back.

She had thought it would have been easy, deadening one's conscience. She believed that a woman's body belongs to her and she can do what she wants with it. It had been fun living for six months in Shavi, and she hadn't raised any objection when those "innocents" had made the mistake of thinking

166

that she was Mendoza's wife and that Dorf was her son. In Shavi, for the first time, she had discovered that she was capable of a depth and concentration of passion that she hadn't suspected. It had gone on and on for weeks, so that she wouldn't have minded if they had never repaired the Newark. But Andria had wanted Kisskiss to have a "civilised" education, not that available in the changing and dusty desert. Well, she didn't blame her. And since that was the case, Flip had worked harder on the Newark, refining the date oil to give them enough fuel to reach Europe.

If the Shavians had paired her with Flip, she would have kept the child, even if Flip hadn't wanted it. But Mendoza was one of those people one liked to know but not really be involved with. He could be so obscenly loud and showy, it made something inside one recoil. He knew about the child. And when she told him that she wouldn't be keeping it, he wasn't even bold enough to protest. He just stared at her, and became cold. Well, it was her life, and her body. By the standard of the age, she'd done the right thing.

But had she? If so, why was she feeling the guilt? And why had she felt a little jealous when Andria, Flip and Kisskiss had come to see her only yesterday? Andria was glowing and as for Flip, he'd forgotten all about going back to help the Shavians. He felt he'd done all he could for them, seeing to it that Asogba was given the agricultural training that would enable him to reform Shavi and that he got a fair reward from the stones they had discovered. Flip didn't feel guilty at all that he had in a way disturbed the Shavians' quiet life. He was an academic and a scientist. His work was to invent, to discover, and that was where his responsibility ended. If people like Mendoza could exploit the discoveries he had made, that didn't bother him. He couldn't be a jack of all trades.

That Europe had not blown herself up confirmed Flip's belief in the Almighty. He had done such a wondrous work in creating the world, that He wouldn't see it destroyed. As far as he personally was concerned, he felt like a man who had been given another lease of life. He had never seen Andria so happy and knew that he'd made the right decision. Now he could leave his research station and drive home, knowing that there was really a home waiting for him, not just a tidy flat with a faint smell of polish which the housekeeper had left. Now Kisskiss's noises, Andria's music, and the ever-present smell of coffee, all meant home. Well, no-one knew how long this would last, but for the moment, with his own child coming, he knew that he still had something to offer. He had Shavi to thank for this. He had thought his career was enough, but after wandering in the desert for days, and coming home to the welcome the women gave him, he knew that humans are communal at heart. He had decided then that he would marry Andria. The notion that love was enough was too academic to be human. He didn't want to go into the pros and cons, anyway. If it were a sin to be so deliriously happy, he hoped God would forgive him. But his happiness showed in his stride, in his confidence, and in his work.

Ista knew that Flip didn't approve of what she'd done. She also knew that, but for Andria, he wouldn't have come to see her. Andria must have insisted. Flip had asked her why she didn't want a child, when she could take care of it even if she didn't want Mendoza. Thousands of women with little or no income had done it and were still doing it. So why hadn't she kept the baby? Flip's self-righteous moralising had annoyed her intensely, and she'd snapped at him to mind his own business. Yet her mind dwelt obsessively on that very question. Was she going to go on worrying about an unborn child for the rest of her life? The gynaecologist had hinted that she had left the abortion rather late. She'd said that she hadn't known the pregnancy was so advanced, and had gone ahead anyway. It was a disturbing surprise to feel as she now felt. Could she go back to work in the hospital and deliver other people's children without regretting her own?

The bird outside twittered irrelevantly as Ista tossed in bed, unable to rest. Maybe she would return to Shavi and use her skills to improve their lives. But they already had so much, in the ceremonies and rituals that dignified their lives, the communal life-style which gave a place to everyone. And could she interfere with their methods of childbirth, now she'd seen how effective they were? Life could be so simple, with women plaiting each other's hair at the end of the day, old people telling stories, women singing to their children, while the men sat in council. Everybody was catered for.

So what did she think she could teach them? No, she could only go there to learn, to study their ways. Maybe if she could understand that way of living, she could teach her own people that there was another way to live. Then she remembered something Flip had said yesterday about Mendoza and the stones they had brought back. It seemed they could be used as industrial diamonds. He wasn't sure whether they would be tough enough, but meanwhile Mendoza had got the monopoly on importing them from Asogba. If they were durable, they could make Shavi rich.

The thought made Ista shout aloud in the empty room. "How rich, my God, how rich? Rich enough to make the same mistakes as us? It would be no better than a rape!"

21
New Shavi

The people of Ongar were wondering what had happened to the quiet cattle sellers from Shavi. Dealers milled around wringing their hands. First there were the signs of imminent and severe drought, meaning that this was the time to buy enough cattle to see them through. They all relied on the low prices the Shavians charged. Not only were their prices good, but they used the money from cattle sales to buy water containers made of camel skin and sometimes the treated skins of camels for covering their bigger houses. It was a very profitable trade. If for one reason or the other they didn't come to this important market, many smaller groups of people would suffer. How would they survive a long drought? They could start eating their camels, but camels were so precious that the Ongar people ate them only as a very last resort. A man who ate his one camel could be said to have eaten his own life. A camel was worth twenty cows.

Just as camels were to the people of Ongar, so cattle were to the Shavians. They wouldn't eat their cows unless there was an unusually important celebration. They saved them for marriages, and as a bride is worth sixteen cows, raising that number to get a wife could be a long term plan. Consequently, most young men in Shavi would start to work very hard early in life to save enough cattle for marriage. Once every six weeks, he could sell one or two to help with the cost of running the

170

household. The Shavians needed the Ongar people, as they too were needed by them.

But the Ongar people looked down on their neighbours because they didn't rear camels. Stories had it that they came originally from south of the big town of Kano, that they were too lazy to be nomads, and they sat behind the hills that gave them shelter, reared cattle and ate goats. Now the market day was well advanced and they hadn't shown up. What then were the people going to do?

The chicken seller saw the sight first. He had two baskets of chickens slung across his shoulders and was shouting for buyers. Suddenly he stopped and started to squawk like the birds he was carrying. "They're coming, they're coming, the shy ones are coming."

People stopped to listen, partly because the heat had now become a burden. One could smell the sweaty parched bodies of animals and humans being almost roasted alive. This would usually have been the time of the midday sleep, except that it was market day. The chicken seller shouted again and excitement spread like a slow wave.

"Fancy making all this fuss just for those stupid cattle rearers," said a voice from the market crowd. This remark was greeted by the easy languid laughter of the rich camel sellers.

They all stood watching as the figures of the Shavian men became clear in the distance. The market people could see them, but no cows. They could even see some camels, no small surprise.

"They're not bringing their cattle. What's happened to them?" the chicken seller asked no-one in particular. He was pushed aside by a more energetic and curious person who had been anxiously waiting all day to buy ten cows for his family.

Asogba's men didn't give them much time to consider. As soon as they were in range, they opened fire on the unsuspecting crowd. Panic spread like locusts. People ran helter skelter

171

whilst the men of Shavi kept on shooting. One or two bold men on camels shot their arrows, and a few tried to get out their fighting knives, but what were those compared to a surprise attack by men armed with machine guns?

Before the evening set in, Asogba and his men had acquired almost fifty camels, frightening off all the people of Ongar, and wounded two people. It was lucky they couldn't shoot any better, for they could have killed many. But those in the market had time to take cover before Asogba's fighting men came too close. After the attack, the Shavians turned back, and made their way to where Asogba had hidden his motor car. All his men had acquired camels and rode like kings by his side.

It was indeed a strange sight. Asogba sat in his Land Rover, his head cloth flying in the cool wind of the evening, his car blowing up a great wake of dust. The camel riders, on their frightened animals, were a little way behind, singing Shavi kora songs, including their song of freedom.

"Now everybody will know that we Shavians aren't so stupid," Viyon, Asogba's half brother, shouted to him. Those who heard him nodded, singing as they rode happily to the next village to repeat their success.

Life however soon became difficult for Asogba and his soldiers, with the slaves they were beginning to take. Many villagers, unable to bear to see their houses burnt, or their camels taken, would give him those relatives that had committed atrocious acts in their community. These troublesome slaves, together with his soldiers, had to be fed. His brother Viyon first taxed Asogba on this point.

"Hmmm, and the drought isn't helping matters," Asogba mused.

"I'm afraid not," Viyon agreed.

"We'll make a strong attack on that village bordering Blimer tomorrow. Tell the men to get ready. I'm sure we'll get food from them. I don't think we should worry that much.

We want the desert to know of our existence, so when the kriors sing of Shavi they will always say that the sons of Pata-yon made Shavi great. Think of that, Viyon, and tell it to our fighting men,'' Asogba said confidently.

But the people of Blimer knew that Asogba and his men were near their village. They had no food to spare, and they couldn't part with their camels. They had neither villains nor extra children to give away, so they packed and rolled their tents and moved to another site.

When Asogba and his men arrived there in great hope, they were surprised and disappointed to see a waste land, with the poles of recently dismantled tents. There wasn't even a drop of water in the water hole, it had all been siphoned away. Asogba then ordered, ''Start killing the camels''.

With the water and meat from the first camel killed, they could survive a few days, which they needed for rethinking.

''Our men aren't just hungry, my Prince, they're longing to see their families and friends. They're getting worried as to how their loved ones are faring in this drought. It will be necessary for us to go back to Shavi to replenish our supplies if we wish to continue with our conquest of the desert,'' said Viyon.

Asogba laughed at first. ''The albino, Mendoza, supplies our families with food and he promised to send tools for dig-ging more waterholes. The timid people of Blimer may be suf-fering from the drought, but our people are safe. Do you think I would be stupid enough to leave our land if I thought that they would come to harm?''

A few days later Viyon warned again that even the camels were getting tired, and the water they had was running dan-gerously low.

''This time, Viyon, I agree with you. After taking that tiny village in Koo, we'll go back to our people with all our con-quests. We're running out of ammunition, and it's apparent that the men long to eat food cooked by their wives and mothers. And my land boat needs oil.''

They got ready in the usual way the following morning and made a surprise attack on Koo, hoping to go back northwards through the gaps in the Tibesti hills, which had given their ancestors protection for generations.

What they didn't bargain for, for the second time, was that word had gone round that they were on their way home. The people of Koo knew that they could reach Shavi no other way. The villagers allowed them to come in the early morning, when it was mercifully cool, but as they started to shoot, they saw to their horror that the whole place was on fire. Each one that tried to escape found a desert knife in his back. The car caught fire and exploded, and camels choked and died. Asogba had miscalculated. The people of Koo hadn't bothered to defend themselves, they had simply run at the sound of the Shavian guns, set fire to their village and waited. Asogba and his men were caught in the fire.

It was a humiliating experience after the successes of the previous months. And it was even more disgraceful when their attackers didn't bother to show themselves. Some people said that the people of Koo had been helped by their own albinos, because at one point, Asogba knew that they were also using guns.

Asogba, badly burned and shaken, survived, as did his brother, Viyon, and six others. They had to make their tortuous way home, through the dry sands up to the hills of Shavi. It took them over twenty days of painful trekking.

During most of this time, Asogba was telling his brother Viyon, who was still listening to him, ''You'll see, we'll re-equip ourselves, and we'll regain all we have lost, camels and slaves. Then we'll go down through Kano and Kokumas to avenge the wrongs they did to our ancestors.'' His few remaining followers simply nodded. If they thought his dreams were the ravings of a madman, they were too weak or tired to say. They kept chewing in silence the dried camel meat they had managed to save from the fire. When they arrived in Shavi, it was in the middle of the day. There was little air and the sun was merciless. Everything looked parched, and the stones were so hot that they burnt their sandals. There was no sound of birds or animals and no sign of the palace guards. It was ghostly.

Asogba and his few remaining soldiers went in cautiously. They didn't know why they had to tread this carefully, but they did. A naked child ran out of a tumbledown dwelling, and screamed on seeing them as if he had seen a ghost. A woman, more like a skeleton than a human being, peeped out of the door. When she saw Asogba and his men, she simply stood there, blinking in the strong light as if she had completely lost her faculties.

"Look, our Prince, is that not Ayi's daughter, the last of the King's queens? What is she doing outside the palace? The King our father has not died...?" Viyon's harsh voice cut through to Asogba.

One or two other women, on hearing their voices, came out to stare. Like Ayi's daughter, they all looked like walking skeletons.

Asogba, who could bear the skull-like stare of the women, no longer, summoned all the energy of his body and cried, "Where's the council of the Elders? I know that there is a drought, but they should be in council, and you should have enough to eat. The albinos sent food..."

The women watched him in silence as he shouted and raved. One of them started to laugh croakily, frightening the bystanders. The originator of the laughter was Iyalode, the priestess.

"You ask for the men, Asogba, the great son of Patayon the Slow? Come, I will show you where our men are."

175

Without hesitating, the sad little group followed the bent woman. As they came near the lake, the strong smell of rotting flesh hit them. Still laughing her ghostly laughter, Iyalode croaked. ''There they are, meeting and making predictions as to how many camels you will bring us.''

Asogba followed her shaky finger and saw a sight that revolted him so that he covered his face and almost ran away from the scene.

''Who killed the Elders?'' Viyon asked with gritted teeth.

''The drought killed many, and the people of Ongar killed the rest by taunting them and telling them of your 'desert conquests'. This killed all of the thinking men. You know that with them shame kills very fast. The talking men are still around, living and hiding behind the Shavi hills. You took all the men of action with you so we have very few men left.'' Iyalode was able to control her laughter enough to explain all that had happened.

''But why should they die of hunger?'' Asogba still insisted.

Iyalode, her body a fraction of its former size, started to laugh again. She asked Asogba and Egbongbele's son standing by, ''Why do people die of hunger? What a question from our great conqueror!''

Asogba swallowed, but told himself that whatever happened he mustn't let the priestess's taunt kill him. He couldn't afford to die of shame, it was too much of a luxury. He must remedy the wrongs he had done.

''But the albinos, didn't they send food?'' Viyon persisted.

It was then that they turned to see Shoshovi staggering towards them. Asogba was so shocked at seeing her that it didn't occur to him to embrace her. And she, like the other women, had that ghostly, vacant look in her eyes. She looked through Asogba and his soldiers as if they weren't there.

''Asogba, my son, you'll have to start all over again. You've been very foolish. You tampered with the peaceful life we had, and now we've lost all our men, our way of life and our privacy. We have to start all over again. There are no more than fifty men in the whole of Shavi, but we have at least kept all the young children alive. Your duty now, Asogba, son of Shavi, is to help us to survive.

"You allowed the albino people who came begging for help to know our strength, and then you allowed them to rape us, to take all we had and all that made us a people. It is now for you to find a place for the New Shavi. This is your duty. Posterity will forgive you if you do so, but if you allow shame and sorrow to kill you, the future kriors will forever sing your damnation. We have been raped once, don't let us be raped twice."

Asogba could neither cry, nor speak. His badly burned leg ached, as did his head. But all eyes were staring at him. He found his tongue. "But what happened to the bird of fire, that promised to come every six days and bring food?"

"We didn't know about their promise. But when the albino came just after you left, he said his country didn't need the stones from Shavi any more. And you know that we didn't prepare for this drought. Our people say that 'the cloth you possess yourself will shield your nakedness'. It is not good to depend on somebody else to cover your body for you. You took all the men of action away, and most of the rest died of shame. It was too late to grow anything. Men simply died like flies, and the women had to survive as they could."

The drought went on for another two months, and many, many more people died. Asogba became the King of Shavi, ruling over a population of only hundreds instead of thousands. He finally married Ayoko since Shoshovi was sure that time had cured the syphilis which she had caught from Ronje. But Shoshovi was wrong, time couldn't eradicate the albino disease. Ayoko passed it to Asogba, and though he had two more wives after her, none of them had children. Since no-one in Shavi knew the cure, neither Asogba nor his wives lived very long.

It was his half brother Viyon who carried on the Shavian line.

Asogba said to his brother Viyon once, "Why did Ogene create people like us, with nothing to contribute to the rest of humanity?"

Viyon, who had always behaved like Patayon, thought long and hard before he replied. "We have a great deal to give, my King. We showed the albinos how to look after each other, how to be responsible for one another. You said that when you went to their country, they put their visitors, even you, our King, among their criminals. And you said that those of them that came here did so because the cleverest men among then were going to blow up all their people. But when they came to us, we put them in our best guest houses. Do you think that was stupid of us? I think Ogene was teaching us a lesson about our way of life, our civilisation. We don't have to run away. We should go on living the way we used to live, surviving our droughts, cultivating our land. Our adventure into the desert, and the Ogene stones, were a dream and a temptation. No-one can blame you for believing their promises – but it was all a bad dream. See what we have all suffered as a result.

"Remember what the Queen Mother said to you the night we returned. She said that Shavi is the Mother of us all. She has been raped once, and we must never allow her to be raped again."

"Viyon, what exactly is civilisation?"

"I don't know what it is, but we have it, the best of it, and maybe the albino people have theirs too. It is difficult to say."

The two brothers sat there for a a long time, pondering about the future.